Lorenzo and the Pirate

"Skilled is the author who interweaves adventure and history into a rollicking yarn that teaches while it entertains. *Lorenzo and the Pirate* takes the young adult reader into the tangled times of the American Revolution, when Britain was at war with her rebelling colonies. The newest in a series of Lorenzo adventure books by Rick and Lila Guzmán, *Lorenzo and the Pirate* will keep you captivated as history comes alive, through the exciting adventures of Lorenzo and his friends."

—BILL RICHARDSON, GOVERNOR OF NEW MEXICO

Praise for
Lorenzo's Secret Mission
by Lila Guzmán and Rick Guzmán

"The Spanish Johnny Tremain."

—*Houston Chronicle*

"One of the book's strengths is its depiction of the cultural diversity (French, Spanish, Choctaw, etc.) that was vital to the revolutionary cause . . ."

—*School Library Journal*

"Surrender!" a British voice roared from the enemy ship.

"Or we will kill every man."

Lorenzo and the Pirate

By Lila Guzmán and Rick Guzmán

Blooming Tree Press
Austin, Texas

Lorenzo and the Pirate

Rights & Permissions
Blooming Tree Press
PO Box 140934
Austin, TX 78714

Library of Congress CIP Data Available

978-1-933831-15-2 (Hardcover)
978-1-933831-25-1 (Softcover)

Visit www.bloomingtreepress.com
for more information.

Printed in the United States by Versa Press.
Job # 09-07589
Printed on 50 lbs Opaque offset

To our kids,
Jennifer & Jason
Daniel
Victoria

and

Bruce Wells
(1948-2009)

Prologue

Sail-ho!" the lookout yelled from the crow's nest. "Off the port bow!"

Blackie scrambled up the schooner's rigging to get a better look and trained his spyglass on a warship barely visible on the distant horizon. He swept it from bow to stern. It was a typical multi-deck vessel built in the Spanish style. Three banks of windows marked officers' quarters at the stern. One room belonged to the captain; the rest, to officers. Typically, a warship had a crew of a thousand.

It also would have a surgeon.

Blackie stowed his spyglass. Deep in thought, he rubbed his thumb against his lower lip. The Liberty was on its way to the closest port to get medical help. The captain had fallen ill with a disease no one onboard had ever seen before. His right leg was turning black and gave off the odor of rotting flesh. A poison had started at the captain's toes where circulation was weakest and had slowly moved up to the ankle. It would soon work its way through his entire body and kill him. Blackie feared the leg would have to be amputated. For that, he needed a surgeon.

Blackie climbed down the rigging. He headed to the quarterdeck where he stood with his hands laced behind him, his face a stone mask. He was worried about the captain but determined not to let the hands on deck read his concern.

"Have you any knowledge of Spanish?" Blackie asked the boatswain.

"No, sir."

"Does anyone onboard?"

"I believe Mr. Crowe does."

"Tell him to report to me with alacrity."

"With what, sir?"

"With alacrity. It means 'with all due speed.'"

"Aye, sir," the boatswain said, hurrying away.

The word *alacrity* had popped out as if it were a regular part of Blackie's vocabulary. Perhaps it was. For the last eight months, he had struggled to recall something, anything about himself. His life was a blank. He did not even know his real name. Blackie was a nickname the captain had bestowed upon him because he dressed all in black.

"You are either an undertaker or a doctor," the captain had quipped. "Or perhaps a minister of God's gospel."

There was another possibility. He was in mourning. But the devil take him! Blackie could not remember anyone dying. All he knew was that all his clothes were black.

What else did he know about himself? Only the obvious. He appeared to be in his mid-twenties and was in excellent health. He was pale and had an English accent. From time to time, he sang a Methodist hymn.

Had something happened to him in the war? A head injury,

perhaps? Did he have family somewhere looking for him?

Blackie focused on the Spanish flag flying over the warship. Spain and Britain were at war. He did not look forward to setting foot on an enemy vessel, for the moment he opened his mouth, they would hear a British accent.

However, the captain's life was in peril. He had no other option.

Chapter One

Lorenzo Bannister leaned over the quarterdeck railing of the San Juan Nepomuceno and watched it plow the sea. Faster! Faster! he silently chanted as the warship churned up white-crested water.

He was three days out from New Orleans and a long-awaited reunion with his wife, Eugenie. The trip to Cuba had taken seven days, but prevailing winds and sea currents promised to cut two days off the journey home.

That suited Lorenzo just fine.

It was December 15, 1779, and he would be home for Christmas. When he had said good-bye to Eugenie on the New Orleans wharf, she had hinted that she had a special Christmas surprise for him. In Cuba, Lorenzo had bought presents for her as he always did on his travels. One gift was a spider monkey. He hoped it would make a good companion for her when military duty took him away from home.

Lorenzo scanned the cobalt water stretching from horizon

to horizon and saw nothing but sea and sky. He thought he saw a small ship on the horizon, but couldn't be sure. Overhead, wind-filled sails puffed out and propelled the San Juan Nepomuceno through the Gulf of Mexico.

Sailing on one of the world's largest warships was the last place he would normally be, but in the last four months, his life had taken some unexpected turns. At eighteen years of age, he gave up a medical practice with an elderly physician to become a staff officer for General Bernardo de Gálvez, a man like a father to him. Perhaps Lorenzo would return to medicine some day, but for now, it was more important to fight the British and protect his home.

The swarm of activity on the San Juan Nepomuceno amazed Lorenzo. Sailors swabbed the decks, polished brass work, and worked the sails. A sailor scrambled up the rigging like a monkey up a tree while a midshipman hurried past on the way to the back of the ship.

Stern, Lorenzo reminded himself. The back of the ship is called the stern.

A naval officer stood watch on the quarterdeck. He looked glorious in a blue jacket with red cuffs, red lining, and wide red lapels. Gold buttons ran down the jacket front and decorated the cuffs. Matching blue breeches, white stockings, shoes with gold buckles, and a bicorne hat completed the uniform. Like all naval officers, he wore a powdered wig tied with a black ribbon.

Lorenzo was the only army officer onboard, and he felt like a blue jay in a flock of peacocks. His uniform consisted of a simple blue vest and breeches, black boots, and white coat with blue collar and cuffs. He wore a three-cornered hat with a red cockade, the symbol of his rank.

He went down the stairs connecting the quarterdeck to the main deck and paused by the chicken coop. Hens craned their necks through the cage bars and cheeped pitifully.

Lorenzo understood their misery. It was not natural for chickens to sail the high seas. For that matter, it was not natural for him, a major in the Spanish army, to be on a ship.

Should the San Juan Nepomuceno happen upon a British ship, a sea battle would ensue. On land, there were options during combat. On the high seas, there was nowhere to go if the ship sank, except into shark-infested water. A lucky shot to the powder magazine would turn the ship into a hail of splinters. Dodging incoming cannonballs during battle was hardly a sport Lorenzo relished. He had seen sandbags stowed below and knew their purpose. In battle, sailors spread sand on the decks to absorb blood.

If all that were not enough to turn a sane man from the seafaring life, there were hurricanes and pirates to consider.

No, Lorenzo decided. He was a landlubber through and through. His grandfather once told him that Bannisters were navy men. If Lorenzo had his way, that grand old tradition would soon end.

A dark-haired cabin boy named Francisco climbed the ladder from the forecastle to the main deck. He poured water from a bucket into troughs for the caged chickens.

The lad was about twelve years old, tall for his age, and powerfully built. Sun and sea had given his face a well-tanned, healthy look.

Without warning, the ship lurched. Lorenzo stumbled and grabbed the railing.

Francisco, the cabin boy, seized his arm to steady him and gave Lorenzo a wry smile. "Don't have your sea legs yet, sir?"

"I was not meant for the sailing life."

"Sir!" the cabin boy exclaimed, dismayed. "What could be better than sailing into heathen ports and seeing the world? It's a grand life!"

"Not for me," Lorenzo said. "I have as much business on this ship as those chickens do."

"Their journey is at an end," Francisco said. "Today they grace the captain's table."

"Pity. I was growing fond of them." They were the only birds he had seen since leaving Havana harbor. The Gulf of Mexico was vast. They had reached the point where they were too far from shore to see birds. Lorenzo squinted at the cabin boy. "Why did you choose the sailing life?"

"I was raised in Andalucía where it is bone dry. The first time I saw the ocean, I couldn't believe all the water. I fell in love with it."

"You can have it. I hate water."

Francisco looked shocked by the confession. "Surely, Your Mercy must swallow a drop now and then. And I certainly hope Your Mercy takes an occasional bath."

Lorenzo laughed. He liked the way Francisco could joke without crossing the invisible line of respect that separated officers from sailors. "I have good reason to avoid water. Twice, I nearly drowned. Once, in a flash flood. Once, in a hurricane."

Francisco nodded. "That would turn a man against water."

The ship's cook walked up to the chicken coop, grabbed four hens by the legs, and walked off carrying two in each hand.

"No cause for worry, sir," Francisco said in mock seriousness. "You'll see your friends again at eight bells."

"Noon?" Lorenzo guessed.

"Aye, sir."

Little by little, Lorenzo was learning the bell system that regulated everything on the ship. Every thirty minutes on the hour and half hour, a bell tolled, marking the time. Sailors had four-hour watches. In order to time the ringing of the bell, the officer of the deck turned a sand-filled hourglass. Eight bells marked the end of a four-hour watch.

All of a sudden, the lookout in the forward crosstrees shouted, "Ship off the starboard bow."

The officer of the deck swiveled in that direction and scanned the area with a spyglass.

Lorenzo shaded his eyes with his hands and saw a three-masted ship on the far horizon.

The officer of the deck shrugged, stowed his spyglass, and went about his business with an amazing lack of concern.

Francisco seemed to read Lorenzo's mind. "No cause for worry, sir. She's no threat."

"How can you tell?"

"She's too small to take us on. I see but three cannons."

Lorenzo was suddenly glad the San Juan Nepomuceno bristled with cannon on both sides of the ship.

"That's a schooner, sir," Francisco said. "A fast ship. Not weighted down with cargo. She rides too high in the water. There's only one problem, Your Mercy."

"And that would be?" Lorenzo prompted.

"No flag at the mizzenmast. You're supposed to fly a flag to show your nationality."

"And if you don't?"

"Then you're probably a pirate."

Chapter Two

Blackie stood on the Liberty's quarterdeck and studied the San Juan Nepomuceno. Rendering aid in an emergency was a tradition on the high seas. He hoped the Spanish warship would honor the custom. "Send a distress signal," he ordered.

"Aye, sir." The boatswain went to the flag box and retrieved a banner. He hoisted it upside down.

The last time Blackie checked on the captain's condition, he had been shocked to see how fast the black rot had spread. The captain had never been in good health. His frail condition had caught Blackie's eye eight months earlier when they'd met in a tavern in Mobile. Blackie had stepped inside for a pint and a bite to eat. When his eyes adjusted to the dim interior, he spotted an elderly gent at a table bent over a book. He wore an eye patch and had but one arm. The cuff of his threadbare coat was pinned to his sleeve.

The elderly gent glanced up from his reading, noticed

Blackie, and motioned for him to join him.

Blackie hesitated.

The man insisted, waving his good arm dramatically.

To make sure that he was not signaling someone behind him, Blackie glanced around.

The captain mouthed the words "Get over here" and punctuated the order with a swift nod.

Blackie obeyed and was glad he did. They took to each other instantly. After two hours of animated conversation on subjects ranging from the rebellious English colonies to the latest literary fads, the captain asked him to join his crew. Blackie had been with the captain ever since. Losing him would be akin to losing a father.

"You wished to speak with me?"

Startled by the voice, Blackie spun.

Josiah Crowe, the ship's navigator, stood behind him.

Blackie hated the way this man skulked about. There was always a glint in Josiah's eye—as if he were plotting Blackie's death.

It had been the captain's decision to bring Josiah Crowe aboard because they needed an experienced navigator. Blackie had taken an instant, irrational dislike to Crowe, a lean-faced man with devil-blue eyes. Maybe it was his Boston accent or the way he treated his fellow sailors as lesser beings. Maybe it was because of the way he wore his long beard in braids. Whatever the cause, Blackie did not like him.

"Do you speak Spanish?" Blackie asked.

"Yes, I do," Crowe replied, puffing up with pride.

"I am going to the San Juan Nepomuceno to get medical help for the captain. I need an interpreter."

Crowe deflated a bit. "I'm not fluent."

"But you speak Spanish?"

"A few words here and there," the man said cautiously. "I doubt that I would prove useful."

"In the land of the blind, the one eyed-man is king."

Crowe looked momentarily befuddled. "Be that as it may, I would be more useful here."

Leaving Crowe in charge of the ship was foolhardy at best. Given the chance, Crowe would sail off without him. No, indeed! It was imperative that he keep this man at his side where he could keep an eye on him.

"Look, sir!" A toothless sailor pointed to the San Juan Nepomuceno and pulled Blackie from his musings.

The ship was acknowledging the Liberty's emergency by running a signal flag up the mast.

Blackie breathed a sigh of relief. "Hoist the white flag! Ready the longboat!"

Under international law, all ships had to honor the white flag, a request for negotiation.

"You can't trust those diegos," Crowe said. "I say we go in under cover of night, kidnap the surgeon, and bring him back here."

"Don't be ridiculous," Blackie snapped. "We are going to the San Juan Nepomuceno as honorable gentlemen, not as thieves in the night."

Crowe snorted. "This is an enormous blunder."

Perhaps it was. But the captain had taken a chance on him when he needed help. It was time to repay the favor.

*   *   *

Lorenzo and Francisco stood in companionable silence at the ship's rail and trained spyglasses on the pirate ship cruising parallel to them. It stayed out of firing range, but stalked them like a tiger.

The ship had finally shown a flag. It was not the Union Jack. Lorenzo took comfort in the thought. Running into a British warship had been General Gálvez's main concern when he sent Lorenzo to Havana as a special courier.

"If the British capture you," Don Bernardo had said, "they must find nothing in writing. Memorize the following message and deliver it to the Captain General. *The British are still reeling from their defeat at Baton Rouge. General Gálvez wishes to strike Mobile now. He respectfully requests that you send ships and supplies without delay.*"

Lorenzo understood the general's impatience. He wanted to finish the job he had started three months earlier. The capture of Baton Rouge was merely the first battle in a campaign to drive the British from the Gulf of Mexico.

General Gálvez would not be happy with the Captain General's response. He refused to send supplies and troops.

Lorenzo could imagine the general's reaction when he told him the news. He would pace about, mumble to himself, and kick the nearest object in frustration. Lorenzo planned to stay out of the line of fire.

A sudden flurry of activity on the pirate ship drew him back to the present. Pirates moved a boat from the top deck and lowered it over the side.

"Have you ever seen a pirate up close?" Francisco asked.

"Never had the pleasure."

"You're about to meet some. Looks like they're coming for a chat."

An image formed in Lorenzo's mind of ruthless men with bandannas around their heads, large gold earrings dangling from their ears, teeth gripping well-honed knives, and a parrot on the shoulder. So far, he had seen no one aboard the schooner fitting that description. He focused on one pirate in particular: a brown-haired fellow dressed in a black shirt with billowy sleeves and black breeches. He stood on the quarterdeck by the ship's wheel and appeared to be in charge.

Lorenzo snapped open his pocket watch to check the time. It was almost noon, time for the changing of the watch. Lorenzo turned, leaned his elbows on the rail, and waited. He enjoyed the shipboard ritual and found it odd and amusing.

A boatswain stood on the forecastle with a silver whistle in hand.

Nearby, a navigator hunched over a table figuring the ship's position on a chart. Computations complete, he walked aft to the officer of the watch and reported the latitude and longitude. "It is now twelve o'clock," he declared.

The officer of the watch, a sour-looking lieutenant in an ill-fitting uniform, turned to the captain and reported the time and the navigator's readings.

"Make it twelve!" the captain told the officer of the watch.

Even though the mate of the watch was within earshot, the officer of the watch called out, "Make it twelve!"

The mate of the watch sang out to the quartermaster, who was also within earshot, "Strike eight bells."

The quartermaster, as solemn as a judge on the bench, said, "Turn the glass and strike the bell."

The sailor on duty did as ordered.

At the sound of the bell, the boatswain put the silver whistle to his mouth and piped a message to everyone within earshot that the four-hour watch was officially over.

Fresh sailors came on deck to replace duty-weary ones. Some scrambled up the rigging while others scrambled down. All of a sudden, one of them missed his footing.

Lorenzo watched in helpless horror as the man plunged downward. His foot caught in the rigging fifty feet above the deck. Hanging upside down, he tried to curl his body up to grasp onto something to pull himself up. That made his foot dislodge. Screeching in terror, he tumbled downwards, arms flailing like windmill blades. He did a half-turn as he fell and bounced off a boom. He hit the deck with a thud.

Lorenzo raced toward the sailor lying in front of a ladder. He pushed his way through men crowded around him and fell to his knees at his side.

The injured man's eyes were closed. He did not move.

Lorenzo prayed that he had only had the wind knocked out

of him. He pressed two fingers to the injured sailor's neck and determined that the fall had not killed him. He glanced over his shoulder and searched for Francisco.

"Get my medical bag, Francisco! It's in my cabin."

"Aye, sir!" The boy bolted away.

Lorenzo did a quick assessment of the patient. His right arm lay at an odd angle, obviously broken. Blood gushed beneath him.

A broken arm was not life threatening. The first order of business was to find the source of the bleeding and stop it. Lorenzo peeled away the man's bloody smock. At some point in the fall, a rod had pierced his side, leaving a hole from front to back.

While Lorenzo waited for the cabin boy to return with his medical bag, he pressed his hand over the wound to stop the blood. It bubbled beneath his palm and seeped through his fingers. Lorenzo pressed down a little harder. He took a handkerchief from his pocket and eased it into the back of the wound.

"Find the ship's surgeon," Lorenzo said to a nearby sailor. "Tell him there has been an accident and he is needed on the quarterdeck. He should be in sickbay."

If he has slept off his hangover, Lorenzo silently added. He shared a cabin with the medical officer. The man had stumbled in blind drunk at three o'clock in the morning after a night of gambling with the midshipmen.

The injured sailor, face contorted in pain, groaned. His eyes opened.

Lorenzo gave him the most comforting smile he could muster. "Your arm is broken and you have a minor wound. It will take about nine weeks for everything to mend. There are easier ways to get out of work, you know."

The sailor smiled weakly, seeming to realize that Lorenzo was using humor to lighten the situation.

Francisco returned carrying both of Lorenzo's medical bags. One was a leather case that contained medicine and bandages. The other was a larger, square box with surgical instruments.

"Open the smaller bag," Lorenzo told Francisco, "and hand me a cloth."

Francisco obeyed.

Lorenzo wiped the blood from his hands. He took out a spoon and a bottle of laudanum, the strongest painkiller in his medical kit. He measured out a dose. Meanwhile, a sailor lifted the wounded man's head and Lorenzo put the spoon to his lips.

Where was the ship's surgeon? What was taking so long?

"Bring me a piece of rope," Lorenzo said to the closest sailor.

He returned with the requested item and handed it to him.

"I'm going to set your arm," Lorenzo said. "Bite down on this." He put the rope in the man's mouth.

"What the hell are you doing, Bannister?"

Lorenzo looked up. The ship's surgeon, arms folded over his chest, glared down at him. He reeked of cheap cologne to mask the fact that he had been drinking before noon. Lorenzo noticed the surgeon had failed to address him as Major or Doctor, but decided to ignore the snub. He stood and explained the patient's situation.

"I was about to set his arm," Lorenzo said in conclusion.

"I'll take it from here," the surgeon said. "Shove off."

Lorenzo yielded to him. The ship was his domain, not Lorenzo's. He picked up his medical bags and blended into the crowd of sailors. He watched the doctor set the arm, ready to jump in if necessary to prevent harm to the patient. Luckily, the surgeon was sober enough to do the job.

Sailors crafted a makeshift stretcher out of a sail and moved the injured man onto it. They carried him below to sickbay while the rest of the onlookers melted away and returned to work.

The surgeon marched over to Lorenzo. "If you know what's good for you," he snarled, "you'll keep your damned paws off my sailors!"

"As a doctor, it is my duty to—"

"Doctor? You're no doctor. You're a quack."

Lorenzo's first impulse was to slug the man in the gut. He struggled to control his flash temper. A voice inside his head said, "Walk away." Officers did not engage in fistfights, although this man was asking for it.

He knew why the ship's surgeon did not consider him a real doctor. Lorenzo had never attended medical school. Instead, he had served as his father's medical apprentice and had completed his training under two surgeons at Valley Forge. After a long, cold winter of working in the camp hospital, they had certified him as a doctor. Upon returning to New Orleans, the city council accepted his credentials and allowed him to open a practice with an elderly physician.

The ship's surgeon, on the other hand, had attended medical school in Paris. He liked to remind Lorenzo of that fact.

Lorenzo ran his hand over the smooth leather of his father's medical bag. Inside his head, he heard Papá's soft Virginia accent. "You mustn't let anything interfere with your medical duty. Not professional pride nor fear for your own safety. The patient always comes first."

Lorenzo turned and walked away.

Chapter Three

Lorenzo started to go below to stow his medical bags when he noticed that the pirates' longboat was about to arrive. The cabin he shared with the ship's surgeon was the size of three coffins placed side-by-side. Lorenzo looked for reasons to stay away from it. Seeing pirates up close seemed a good reason to loiter on the quarterdeck.

Down in the longboat, ten men worked the oars while one sat in the back at the tiller. Two men, one of them the pirate in black, sat in the bow.

The captain and four officers gathered to greet the longboat's occupants. Armed marines waited by the sea ladder, a series of iron bars fixed to the side of the ship.

The first man out of the boat and onto the quarterdeck was the pirate in black. He raised his hands in a gesture of surrender and turned toward a marine. While being searched for weapons, the pirate's gaze flitted from the captain to the ship's surgeon and the naval officers flanking him.

A feeling of unease budded inside Lorenzo. The pirate reminded him of someone. He had cream-colored skin, dark blue eyes, and short brown hair. Self-assurance radiated from him, as if he could be the master of any situation. Lorenzo could not shake the feeling that they had met before and that it had not been a pleasant experience.

"No weapons, captain," the marine declared, stepping back into place.

The pirate lowered his hands. In one fluid gesture, he swept the hat from his head, placed it over his chest, and bowed low to the captain.

The captain responded with a curt nod.

A second pirate scrambled up the ladder and joined the first on deck. He, too, was thoroughly searched. The remaining pirates stayed in the boat.

Lorenzo smiled to himself. Now this man, the second pirate, fit his mental image of a pirate, from the strangely braided beard to the cutthroat look in his eye.

"Thank you for answering my distress signal," the first pirate said in English.

The second pirate translated. "*Gracias para respuesta mi señal.*"

The captain frowned, seemingly mystified by the mangled translation. "Welcome aboard," he said in Spanish.

"I am Blackie," the first pirate said, "quartermaster of the Liberty, and this gentleman is Mr. Crowe, my navigator."

The translator said, "*El se dice que se llama es Blackie, jefe*

21

del barco Liberty. Me llamo Señor Crowe, el navigator."

The captain's frown deepened as he tried to decipher the words. "What is the nature of your emergency?"

Blackie turned to the other man expectantly.

The second man seemed at a loss.

Seeing their dilemma, Lorenzo set his medical bags down and left the railing where he had been watching everything. He approached the captain from behind and whispered in his ear, "Pardon the intrusion, sir, but I speak English."

"For God's sake," the captain whispered back, "translate what these two are trying to say. I can make neither head nor tail of it."

"Gentlemen," Lorenzo said, addressing the two pirates, "the captain wishes me to serve as translator."

"You speak English," Blackie said, clearly relieved. "Please thank your captain for answering our distress signal."

Lorenzo translated.

"Ask them the nature of their emergency," the captain said.

Lorenzo did as ordered.

"Our captain has fallen ill," Blackie said. "His leg is turning black. I fear it must be amputated soon or his life will be forfeit."

Lorenzo explained the situation to the captain.

"Tell them they may bring him onboard for medical treatment," the captain said.

Blackie shook his head. "Moving my captain would be the death of him, sir. He is too weak. A physician will have to travel to him."

Upon hearing the translation, the ship's surgeon stiffened. "I am not going on a pirate ship!"

Blackie needed no translation. Disappointment was written on his face. "Please," he begged, hands outstretched pleadingly.

"No!" the surgeon said, shaking his head vigorously. "I will not waste my skills on a pirate."

"For the love of God," Lorenzo said, "you're a doctor."

"The damned fellow has a cook onboard," the surgeon said. "Have him cut the man's foot off."

Lorenzo stared at the surgeon in dismay. "You can't deny him medical care just because he's a pirate."

"I most certainly can."

"No, you can't!"

Blackie tilted his head and lifted his hands questioningly, clearly confused by the discord between Lorenzo and the surgeon.

Lorenzo turned to the captain. "Sir, I would like to go."

"Indeed you shall not!" The captain looked appalled by the suggestion.

"Sir, I—"

"Major Bannister," the captain said curtly, "a word with you please." He stepped away from the knot of officers.

Lorenzo dutifully joined him. He braced himself for a dressing down. It was bad form to argue with a fellow officer. It was even worse form to argue with a superior officer.

"Young man," the captain said, leaning close to Lorenzo, "I cannot permit you to put yourself in danger. General Gálvez will place my head on a pike if something happens to you."

"Nothing will happen. It's in their best interest not to harm me."

"I could order you not to go."

"Yes, sir, you could. But do you wish to have a man's death on your conscience?"

"Better his than yours."

"Sir, do you recall yesterday's homily?"

The captain did not answer. He regarded Lorenzo through narrowed eyes. The day before when the ship's chaplain celebrated mass on the main deck, he had based his homily on the Good Samaritan and had focused on helping others.

"This is a chance to put principle into action," Lorenzo said. "Sir, I can go to the pirate ship, take care of the patient and return before nightfall."

"Bah! It will be a waste of breath to try to talk you out of this folly. Go be a Good Samaritan. Just don't get yourself killed."

Lorenzo merely smiled. Part of him agreed that this was folly. Another part of him said he was doing the right thing.

Side by side, he and the captain headed to the cluster of pirates, marines, and naval officers. To Lorenzo's surprise, the captain veered to the railing and looked down at the pirates waiting for the return of their shipmates. He bounced his palm lightly on the railing as if a sudden thought had come to him. "Who are the three youngest men in the longboat?" The captain directed the question to Blackie.

Startled, he hesitated. "Tim Pennington, Andy Smith, and

Stephen Caldwell."

"Their ages?"

"Fourteen, seventeen, and twenty."

"Tell them to come aboard."

Blackie frowned, but obeyed.

Three rosy-cheeked young men in billed caps climbed the sea ladder. Looking acutely uncomfortable, they stood on the quarterdeck and allowed the marines to search them.

Blackie cleared his throat and tapped his head. Understanding the silent order, the three young sailors took off their caps and held them over their chests.

The captain laced his hands behind his back. His gaze burned a path to Blackie. "Major Bannister is a physician. He has agreed to go to your ship to tend to the captain. You may have the good doctor's services for five hours. These three fine fellows and your navigator will stay in the hold until his return."

There was a pause while Blackie digested that. "As you wish, Captain. You have my pledge that Major Bannister will return unharmed." He turned to his sailors. "Be good, honest fellows. Do not cause the captain any grief."

"Aye, sir," they said in unison.

He stretched out his hand to the navigator. "Until we meet again, Mr. Crowe."

Crowe shot Blackie a murderous look as he took his hand and gave it a limp shake.

Lorenzo climbed down the sea ladder to the waiting pirates.

Chapter Four

On the way to the Liberty, Blackie sat in the bow across from Major Bannister and studied this strange man who had willingly put himself in peril. He spoke in a cultured dialect that suggested a good education, a good up-bringing, and good connections.

Blackie had seen the name "Bannister" recently. But where? It suddenly struck him. A few months ago, he posted a letter for Captain Slaughter that was addressed to someone named Bannister. What was the first name? It was an odd one that began with an A.

"What's your first name?" Blackie asked.

The doctor looked surprised by the question. "Lorenzo."

That was not the name on the letter.

Why did this chap have an English last name? He looked completely Spanish, with dark skin, black eyes, and straight black hair. Irishmen had joined the Spanish army in droves, but this man bore no resemblance to people from the Emerald Isle.

Overcome by curiosity, he asked, "Where did you learn English?"

"My father was a Virginian."

"Ah! That accounts for the accent."

"Accent? I don't have an accent."

"Indeed you do. It smacks of treason."

"Treason or liberty?"

Blackie chuckled. "I suppose that depends on which side of the pond you live on."

For some reason, the most influential rebels hailed from Virginia. There was Mr. Washington, the commander in chief of the Continental Army. Thomas Jefferson, who had written the Declaration of Independence. And Blackie's personal favorite, Patrick Henry, a troublemaker always stirring the people to rebellion.

Under the current climate, politics was a dangerous subject. Upsetting the doctor before surgery was not a good idea. Blackie searched for a different topic of conversation. "Where did you study medicine?"

"I apprenticed under my father, the fellow who taught me to speak English with an accent."

Blackie laughed.

The sailors rowing the longboat exchanged glances of amusement, evidently admiring the doctor's quick wit.

"Which title do you prefer?" Blackie asked. "Doctor or Major?"

"Either one will do. What shall I call you?"

"Blackie."

"Do you have a last name?"

"Blackie will suffice."

"And my patient's name?"

"Captain Slaughter."

"Is that his real name?"

"As real as 'Blackie.'"

The doctor smiled wanly. A sudden breeze from the south stirred the sea and gently rocked the longboat. Dr. Bannister clutched its side with one hand and the edge of his seat with the other.

Blackie smiled to see a crack in the man's composure. This little puff of air was nothing compared to gale-force winds that howled like a lost soul and tossed ships to and fro.

"How long has the captain been ill?" Dr. Bannister asked.

"Several weeks."

"You said his foot has turned black."

"Yes. It looks like gangrene has set in."

"Did he injure his foot?"

"No. It just started turning black."

"How long has it been that way?"

"I don't know. The captain is not the kind of man to complain or draw attention to himself."

"What are his other symptoms?"

"He urinates too frequently and constantly asks for water. He says his mouth stays dry. I've served under his command for eight months. He has never had a strong constitution, but now he has no appetite. He grows weaker by the day."

"How old is he?"

Blackie thought about that. "I'm not sure. Maybe sixty."

"What is his urine like?"

"Pardon me?" Blackie said.

"His urine. Is it thin and pale? Is there a pleasant smell to it?"

"Yes to both questions."

"Is the captain slow to heal?"

Blackie was taken aback. All the doctor's questions were spot on. "Yes. He cut his finger once and it took forever to heal."

"I see," the doctor said, his gaze going to the far horizon.

"Do you know what's wrong with the captain?"

"I don't want to make a diagnosis until I've had a chance to examine him." The doctor glanced away to rain-laden clouds moving in from the south and scowled.

Blackie followed his line of sight to the veil of rain where sky and sea met.

*   *   *

A knot tightened in Lorenzo's stomach to see clouds marching across the sky. Wave after wave struck the longboat and made it buck like a bronco. The wind seemed stronger now and the water choppier. To take his mind off his misery, Lorenzo concentrated on the pirate opposite him. He sat with perfect posture, staring straight at Lorenzo, studying him as if sizing him up for a coffin.

The longboat docked, and Lorenzo climbed a rope ladder to the deck.

Lorenzo's appearance on the schooner brought work to a halt. Pirates stared at him as if he were an exotic bird that had landed onboard.

"Mind your manners, gentlemen," Blackie said, "and stop gawking at Dr. Bannister." He clapped his hands. "Back to work!"

All obeyed, except a ten-year-old boy swabbing the deck. He dropped his mop and raced over. "Mr. Blackie, sir, where's my brother?"

"Not to worry, son," he said, placing a hand on the boy's shoulder. "He's on the San Juan Nepomuceno. I shall fetch him when I return the good doctor."

The promise seemed to satisfy the boy. He returned to swabbing the deck.

"The captain is in his cabin," Blackie said to Lorenzo. "Follow me." He led him down a companionway ladder and paused in front of a door elaborately carved with ivy and lilies. He swung the door open and motioned Lorenzo inside.

He ducked into the room.

A boy about Francisco's age sat in a chair picking at his fingernails. The second he saw Blackie, he shot out of his chair and stood at attention. "G'day, sir," he said.

"Hello, Abercrombie. Any change in his condition?"

"No, sir. He fades in and out."

"When was the last time you ate?"

"Before you went a-visiting."

"Go to the galley and eat something."

"Aye, sir."

Lorenzo looked around the captain's room. It was spacious, about six feet long and nine feet wide. To the right, tucked into a corner, was a single berth with a chest of drawers beneath it. The captain lay in bed, a blanket tucked under his chin, a patch over one eye.

Four large windows wrapped around the back of the room and offered a panoramic view of the sea. It was comforting to see the San Juan Nepomuceno sailing beside them.

The room gleamed with luxury. Its elaborately carved cabinets, chairs and chests were made of teak. On one counter rested a razor, washbasin, and a porcelain pitcher. Every inch of space was used wisely. The room smelled clean. Lorenzo saw no signs of roaches or rats. He had dined with the San Juan Nepomuceno's captain in his cabin. These accommodations rivaled anything Lorenzo had seen there.

Blackie put the back of his hand to the captain's brow and frowned. "He still has a slight fever." He took his pulse. His movements were fluid and natural, as if they were second nature. He bent over a piece of paper on the chart table and made a notation. He handed Lorenzo the paper.

Lorenzo scanned it. The detailed entries gave basic statistics on the patient's pulse, temperature, coloring and other astute observations. Blackie had even drawn the captain's foot and leg showing the gangrene's day-by-day advance.

Lorenzo was impressed. It was a better system than the one he used to track a patient's progress.

Blackie must have seen his look of surprise. "Last week, when I realized how serious his foot had become, I began taking notes on his condition."

Lorenzo lifted the cover to examine the captain's leg. It was swollen twice the normal size and looked like it might burst at any moment.

The captain suffered from an advanced stage of gangrene. There was only one thing to do—amputate.

Chapter Five

"What's your diagnosis?" Blackie whispered to Lorenzo.

"He has diabetes," Lorenzo whispered back. "I'll have to amputate."

"Talk a little louder," the captain mumbled. "I can barely hear you." His good eye fluttered open and fixed on Lorenzo. "Who are you?"

"I'm a doctor," Lorenzo said, smiling down at him. "Blackie brought me here."

"Where is the scoundrel?"

Blackie stepped forward. "Here, Captain."

"The devil take you!" he growled. "Why did you bring a doctor? I'll die soon enough without having a leech around."

"Captain!" Blackie said in an admonishing tone. He offered Lorenzo an apologetic smile.

"I've been called worse," Lorenzo said. At the camp hospital, pain-ridden soldiers often cursed at him.

"That a Spanish uniform?" the captain asked.

"Yes, sir."

"Thought so." With that, the captain appeared to fall asleep.

"Under normal circumstances," Blackie said, "my lord and master is a very nice fellow who minds his manners."

This time Blackie did not whisper and Lorenzo understood that the statement was more for the captain than for him.

Lorenzo moved to the far side of the room and gestured for Blackie to join him.

There was a rumbling overhead that sounded like a sailor rolling a barrel on deck. Lorenzo prayed it was not thunder. Beyond the window, clouds heavy with rain swallowed the sun and slowly erased the sky.

"Diabetes is not a death sentence," Lorenzo said. "He can live for a long time with it."

"Have you treated it before?"

"Many times." Lorenzo paused. "After the operation, I'll discuss the captain's diabetes with you further. I have a medical book in my bag with a chapter on the disease. You may find it enlightening."

Blackie nodded. "I am sure I will. The ship is at your disposal. What will you need for the amputation?"

"A place to operate. This cabin is too small," Lorenzo said.

"The best location would be the top deck. I'll have to clear a space."

"I need a table about this far off the ground." Lorenzo measured a distance of four feet.

"The ship's carpenter can put the death board on some barrels."

"What's a death board?"

"It's the thing we use for burial at sea."

"I see."

Lorenzo picked up his medical bags and headed to the companionway. He stopped halfway up. Rain peppered the deck. An eerie gray light stretched from horizon to horizon.

"What's wrong?" Blackie asked.

"It's raining. I'll have to operate somewhere else."

"There's a table in the galley," Blackie said.

He led Lorenzo to a room where four pirates were playing cards and smoking. They sat at a table about five feet long and four feet wide located in the center of the room. Abercrombie, the cabin boy, was finishing a plate of sausage and beans. Along the far wall, a fire burned in a brick oven. A steaming kettle hung from a hook inside it.

Upon seeing Blackie, the pirates rose.

"This will do," Lorenzo said.

"Stand guard at the door, Zach," Blackie said to a redhead about fourteen years old. "The galley is closed until further notice." He turned to Lorenzo. "Dr. Bannister, you may do with it as you will."

"You," Lorenzo said, picking two sailors at random. "Clear the table and place the benches beneath it. And you, sweep the floor."

The sailors frowned and looked at Blackie as if they expected him to countermand the order.

"Don't make him ask twice," Blackie said. "An order from this gentleman is the same as an order from me."

Without another word, the men set to work.

In his mind's eye, Lorenzo reconstructed the operating room at Valley Forge. "Bring me two small tables, all the sponges you can find, a wash basin, a water pitcher, towels, a bucket of water, a pillow, and blankets."

The remaining sailors scampered off to scavenge for the requested objects.

While Lorenzo waited, he closed his eyes and traced a cross from forehead to chest. He silently recited a prayer. Two years earlier, he had assisted at an amputation, but he had never done one on his own. It was one thing to watch. It was another matter entirely to be in charge of cutting off a man's limb. He opened his eyes to find Blackie lighting lanterns bracketed to the wall.

"If God is with us," Blackie said, "who can be against us?"

A pirate who quoted the Bible. Hardly what Lorenzo expected.

He looked out a porthole. The sky was charcoal. It was far too early to be so dark. He had prayed for strength to perform the operation. Perhaps, he thought, I should have also asked for clear skies.

Two of the pirates returned with the small tables Lorenzo had asked for. He had one placed at the foot of the amputation table and the other by the oven.

A pirate entered with an armload of towels.

Lorenzo took two and spread them on the small tables. He hung a number of towels from hooks fixed in the ceiling beams and ordered the rest stashed on benches beneath the large table.

Pirates appeared at the door bearing the rest of the items. Lorenzo placed a tin basin on the small table by the oven and arranged sponges at regular intervals.

"What can I do?" Blackie asked.

"Take the instruments out of my surgical kit and place them on the other table."

Out of the corner of his eye, he watched Blackie snap open the latches to the surgical kit and lay out a screw tourniquet, amputation saw, scalpels, and straight and curved amputation knives. He removed a tenaculum, an instrument with a wooden handle and a hook at one end, and placed it on the towel. Next came needles, thread, and a piece of worsted tape.

For a long moment, Blackie studied the arrangement, decided the scalpel and the tenaculum were out of order, and moved them. He reminded Lorenzo of a butler fussing over place settings before a fancy dinner.

Lorenzo noted that he had not taken out the retractor or the bullet probe. Those were used to pull back the edges of a wound and locate musket balls. Evidently, he knew they would serve no useful purpose in an amputation.

To be more comfortable during the operation, Lorenzo took off his jacket and handed it to a pirate who folded it carefully and looked for a place to stash it. Seeing none, he left the room.

Lorenzo searched through his medical bag and took out laudanum. He put it next to the surgical instruments.

Blackie picked it up and shook his head. "The captain will not take that."

"Why not?"

"He does not wish to become an opium addict."

Lorenzo contemplated that. Addiction was an unfortunate side effect of the drug. Occasionally, a patient refused to take it, saying the cure was worse than the disease.

"I'll give him whiskey instead."

"There is none onboard," Blackie said.

"Rum?" Lorenzo suggested.

Blackie shook his head.

"What kind of ship doesn't have whiskey or rum?"

"A ship run by a Baptist."

"The man must accept a pain killer," Lorenzo said in exasperation. "An amputation is excruciating without it."

"You can offer, but he will refuse." Blackie smiled ruefully. "I know my captain."

Lorenzo could not force him to take it. This was a complication he hadn't counted on. "Bring in the patient," he said, with a swift nod to the pirates waiting patiently across the table from him.

They left.

He rolled up his sleeves and fished a small scrub brush and a cake of soap from his medical bag. He poured hot water into the basin and set about scouring his hands. As he did so, he noticed Blackie looking on with great curiosity.

"A trick I learned from my father," Lorenzo said.

"Scrub your skin until it bleeds?"

"Wash your hands before you touch a patient."

"Why?"

Lorenzo ignored the question. He did not know why it worked, but it did. Putting his hands up to the light, he twisted them first one way and then the other, examining them carefully. Finding a speck of dirt under a fingernail, he scrubbed at that spot. He held his hands over the washbasin and nodded in Blackie's direction.

Blackie poured water over Lorenzo's hands.

"You make a fine surgeon's mate."

"I'll keep that in mind," Blackie said as he handed him a towel, "should I be dismissed as quartermaster. Come here," Blackie said to a sailor. With the lad's help, he repeated Dr. Bannister's handwashing ritual in case he needed to serve as surgeon's mate during the surgery.

Two sailors carried the captain in a blanket and placed him on the table. They put a pillow under his head and a blanket over him.

He slowly opened his eyes and glanced about. His gaze lingered on the saw and knives before locking on Lorenzo's face.

"There is no way to save your leg," Lorenzo said. "If I could, I would."

Not a flicker of emotion showed on the man's face.

"I want you to take a sedative," Lorenzo said.

"No."

Lorenzo glanced at Blackie. His expression seemed to say *I told you so.*

"Please take a sedative," Lorenzo begged.

"No. Do what you must and be quick about it."

"I will do my best," Lorenzo promised. He recalled that one of the surgeons at Valley Forge could drop a leg in one minute and ten seconds from the moment the knife touched the skin. Lorenzo hoped to match his speed.

"You," Lorenzo said to the sailor called Abercrombie, "stand at his head. You and you," he said, indicating two brawny sailors, "hold his arms." To another man, he said, "Hold his left leg and keep it out of the way." Lorenzo slipped a tourniquet of worsted tape over the doomed leg and positioned it above the knee. He turned the screw that tightened the tape and compressed the artery. Next, he measured four fingers below the kneecap and drew the cutting line. He tied the piece of worsted below it.

The schooner rolled slightly, pitching Lorenzo off balance. He yearned for a floor that did not move. He picked up the scalpel and took a deep breath.

Chapter Six

Blackie saw a glazed look on the doctor's face and instinctively realized he was blocking all emotion for the task at hand.

The captain seemed to be in a waking trance as well. His eyes remained fixed on Lorenzo. The faces of sailors holding down the captain were pinched with absolute terror.

A distant clap of thunder broke the silence. Rain pinged against the porthole.

The boatswain, a sailor with years of experience, was at the helm. If the seas grew rougher, Blackie would head topside.

Dr. Bannister, bending over the captain's leg, drew the scalpel over the flesh at the cutting line. Blood welled up in the gash and trickled down in two bright streams in opposite directions. He cut the outside half, then the inside.

Blackie grabbed sponges and sopped up blood.

Sweat beaded on the captain's forehead. Grabbing a clean towel, Blackie sopped it up as well. Captain Slaughter's eyes rolled back in his head, and he passed out.

Dr. Bannister cut through the muscle to the bone. Suddenly, he stopped and muttered a string of Spanish.

Something had gone wrong. A stab of terror went through Blackie.

"Blackie," Dr. Bannister said, "there's a leather strap in my kit. I need it."

The strap! Of course. It was used to push back muscle and skin in order to expose the bone.

Blackie silently scolded himself for missing it when he fussed over the arrangement of the surgical instruments. Something had seemed out of kilter. On instinct, he had known something—the strap—was missing.

Blackie squeezed past two sailors to get to the bags. He passed the strap to the doctor.

By now, Dr. Bannister had put down the bloody scalpel and was wiping his hands on a towel dangling overhead. He picked up a clean scalpel. Wrinkling his brow in concentration, he placed the piece of leather on the table and made a one-inch slit in the middle of it.

The ship lurched. The scalpel slipped.

Dr. Bannister howled in pain, dropped the scalpel, and grabbed his fingers.

One of the sailors cursed. The others went pale.

"Let me see that," Blackie demanded. He grabbed a towel from overhead and dabbed at the blood welling up. He examined the wound. It was a small cut on the left hand, right below the joint on the middle finger. He rooted around in Dr. Bannister's medical bag until he found a bottle neatly labeled "ointment of calamine." Blackie instinctively knew it was perfect for cuts and burns. He applied it to the wound. Looking up, he saw pain on the doctor's face.

Blackie forced a smile. "What were you thinking, Doc? You will need that finger some day."

The doctor's scowl relaxed to a frown.

Thunder cracked overhead. It sounded closer now and was more frequent.

Blackie tore a strip from a towel and tied it around the finger. "That little accident will leave you with a dandy scar that will impress the girls."

For a couple of seconds, Dr. Bannister merely stared at him before his usual good humor resurfaced. He smiled and looked at his wounded hand. "Shall we return to the matter at hand?"

"Let's," Blackie said, returning the smile.

Dr. Bannister bent over the leg. Lips mashed together, he used the strip of leather to move the muscle out of the way and expose the leg bone.

Blackie suspected the finger was hurting like the devil, but the doctor was too proud to admit it.

"Hand me the saw," the doctor said.

While the saw rasped and chewed on bone, Blackie worked at sopping up blood with the towel.

"Catch it, Blackie," the doctor said as the leg slid off.

Blackie wrapped it in a towel and tucked it on a bench under

the table. "Well done, Dr. Bannister. I could not have done better."
He scooped up a tenaculum. "Shall I close for you?"

The doctor looked shocked by the question. His gaze went
from Blackie to the tenaculum, and back again. "Please."

Blackie hooked an artery, pulled it out a short distance, and
tied it off with thread. He did the same with the others. Finished,
he looked up to see the doctor staring at him, eyes wide, mouth
slightly open.

Perplexed, Blackie looked at his handiwork. It was perfect.
Why was the doctor upset?

"I'll take it from here," Dr. Bannister said in a slightly choked
voice.

Blackie nodded and stepped back. Rain pinging at the porthole drew his attention away from the operation. When he
looked back, the doctor had removed the tourniquet.

Zach, the pirate guarding the door, stuck his head inside.
"Mr. Blackie, sir, storm's coming. Your presence is requested
topside."

"I shall be there in a thrice."

This was the announcement Blackie had dreaded. A storm
at sea was a devilish thing. To hide his concern, he lingered a
moment at the operating table, silently counting to ten. "Good
show, everyone. Dr. Bannister, I am sure I speak for the captain
and crew when I give you my deepest gratitude."

The doctor acknowledged the remark with a nod.

Blackie turned and left. He eased the door shut and bolted
up the companionway.

* * *

Lorenzo finished the operation in something of a daze. Blackie had tied each ligature with a surgeon's knot. The more Lorenzo learned about this fellow, the more convinced he became that he was a doctor. At first, he thought he was a surgeon's mate or a nurse. Based on his actions during the amputation, Lorenzo suspected Blackie could have done the surgery himself. Why hadn't he?

Chapter Seven

General Bernardo de Gálvez sat in his office checking and cross-checking the list of supplies he needed against the list of supplies he had gathered so far. Annoyed by the constant delays, he crumpled the list and flung it to the far side of the room. "*¡Madre de Dios!*" He looked up to find a figure standing in the doorway.

"*Mon amour!*" his wife, Felicité, exclaimed in French, bending over and retrieving the paper. "What a temper!"

He cringed. "How much of that did you see?" he asked in her native language.

"Enough. What has upset you so?"

"The usual."

She closed the door behind her, walked over to his desk, smoothed out the paper, and put it under a paperweight. Smiling sweetly, she sat in his lap and eased her arms around his neck.

He pulled her toward him, and they shared a kiss.

"Feel better now?" she whispered in his ear.

He gave her a sly look. "It's a start. I will feel even better when Lorenzo gets back."

Felicité made a disappointed face. "But then Eugenie will go back to Baton Rouge, and it will be weeks before I see her again."

Gálvez felt a twinge of guilt for interrupting Lorenzo and Eugenie's honeymoon. They had been married only two months when he sent a message to Lorenzo: *Report to me at once.* On the other hand, he had given them a house as a wedding present. That lessened his guilt somewhat.

The two had left Baton Rouge and made their way down the river road to New Orleans, Eugenie's hometown. In Lorenzo's absence, she was staying with the Gálvez family and renewing old friendships.

Gálvez smiled to recall Lorenzo's reaction when he had told him he was going on a secret mission. "Tomorrow at dawn, you leave for Havana."

"That's in Cuba, sir," Lorenzo had pointed out.

"And?"

"Cuba is in the middle of the Caribbean Sea."

"And?"

"The only way there is by ship, unless I sprout wings and fly."

Gálvez had laughed. "I don't care how you get there, Lorenzo."

"You know how I feel about water."

"Look at this as a chance to overcome your fear. Now off with you!"

The next morning, Lorenzo had set sail for Cuba. If all went

47

well, the San Juan Nepomuceno would dock in New Orleans by the end of the week, and Lorenzo would bring a pledge from the Captain General for troops, ships, and supplies. If anyone could pull this off, Lorenzo could.

Felicité slid off her husband's lap. "Eugenie and I are going visiting this afternoon. We should be back around five o'clock." She headed to the door, glanced over her shoulder, and gave him a mock salute. "*Au revoir, mon général.*"

He saluted back. Felicité had put him in a good mood. Marrying her had been the best move of his entire life, even if he had snubbed the king in doing so. King Carlos had been miffed, for a Spanish nobleman was not to marry without his permission, but His Majesty had gotten over it when word arrived that Gálvez had defeated the British at Baton Rouge.

He returned to the problem at hand: ships, supplies and soldiers. He pulled out a map and studied it. He had drained all the soldiers he could from non-traditional sources before Baton Rouge. He moved his finger around the map and sighed. Lorenzo was his best hope.

* * *

Lorenzo slumped into a chair close to the bed where the captain slept. With a storm brewing, returning to the San Juan Nepomuceno would not be possible for a couple of hours.

"The smoking lamp is out!" a youthful-sounding voice announced beyond the cabin door. "The smoking lamp is out!"

Blackie had probably ordered the smoking lamp extinguished as a safety precaution for the approaching storm.

Lorenzo had heard sailors aboard the San Juan Nepomuceno grumble whenever the captain ordered the smoking lamp extinguished. It seemed foolhardy to let sailors smoke in the first place and run the risk of the ship burning down.

Abercrombie entered the captain's cabin. "Begging your pardon, sir." He blew out the lantern bracketed to the wall and left.

A dismal gray settled over the cabin. Lorenzo looked for something to do. To judge by the number of books in the captain's quarters, he liked to read. Lorenzo put his face close to the book spines to make out the titles and discovered that most were religious texts. There were several copies of the King James Bible and a number of hymnals.

Little natural light came from outside, not nearly enough to read by, so Lorenzo returned to his chair. After checking the captain, he settled in for a nap.

Noise beyond the ship walls made sleep impossible. Thunder continued to rumble. It became constant, one boom after the other. It reminded Lorenzo of the roar of cannon as Gálvez bombarded Fort Richmond during the Battle of Baton Rouge.

The ship began to rock back and forth like a cradle.

Lorenzo wedged pillows around the captain to keep him from rolling. The elderly man groaned, opened his eyes, looked at Lorenzo, and fell back asleep.

A mixture of gray rain, fog, and mist obscured the San Juan Nepomuceno. Could Blackie and his sailors see it topside? Or were they sailing blind? What if the Liberty and the warship smacked together? That couldn't be good for either ship, especially the smaller one.

Suddenly, the rain lessened. There were several minutes of calm when nothing happened. Light filtered through patches in the clouds. Lorenzo closed his eyes and let out a long breath. Maybe the storm had blown over.

A long rumble destroyed his illusion. The storm had only taken a break to build up its strength. Now clap after clap of thunder sounded. The heavens opened and dumped buckets of water on the Liberty. Lightning flashed and illuminated first one cloud and then another. At the height of the storm, bolts danced from cloud to sea. Wind drove the rain at a forty-five degree angle.

Lorenzo's stomach lurched and he felt like vomiting. It was bad enough to be on a ship when the weather was good. But in a storm? What if the ship sank? He wondered what was happening topside with Blackie and the crew. He prayed they had everything under control.

The storm tossed the ship forward and back as if two giants were playing tug-of-war with it. Sheer pandemonium broke out in the captain's cabin. Lorenzo dodged books falling off shelves. Chairs and tables overturned. Charts fell off the table. The captain's jacket, hanging from a peg, swayed as if it were dancing a jig. Ink sloshed out of the inkpot on the desk. The drawer under the captain's bed flew out.

Everything not nailed down seemed to move. Small objects rolled back and forth or slid across the floor.

The only thing that stayed in place was a small, padlocked chest in a corner of the room. It looked like the doubloon-filled chest his father described in his stories. Papá had woven elaborate tales of pirates drunk on rum and burying ill-gotten gain on deserted islands. He would be disappointed with these tea-totaling buccaneers. Lorenzo smiled at the thought.

The storm raged on. From time to time, the captain cried out in pain. Lorenzo checked on him, but determined that the man still slept.

When Lorenzo decided that the worst was over, he straightened up the room, putting books back on shelves and righting chairs and tables.

He put the drawer back on its slide bar and was about to push it in when a piece of material made out of familiar colors caught his attention. He pulled it out, disbelieving his eyes, and took it to the window where he examined it in the dim light.

It bore thirteen stripes, alternating red and white, and a blue field with thirteen stars.

"*Dios mío,*" Lorenzo whispered, struck by a sudden thought. Congress had passed a resolution three years earlier allowing private ships to attack the British in the name of the United States. Lorenzo draped the flag over the table and searched through the drawer, looking for a letter of marque. He found it beneath carefully folded socks. It was issued by the Continental Congress and signed by Benjamin Franklin.

Footsteps sounded beyond the door. Lorenzo put the document back. He picked up the flag, but before he could stash it in the drawer, the cabin door opened.

Blackie stepped inside carrying a lantern. A shaft of light fell on the American flag draped in Lorenzo's arms.

Scowling, Blackie took a menacing step forward and placed the lantern in a bracket on the wall. He clucked at Lorenzo. "Too bad you found this. Now I shall have to kill you."

The smile spreading across Blackie's face told Lorenzo he had nothing to fear. He took one end of the flag and Lorenzo, the other. Together, they folded it. Blackie took it from him, squatted by the drawer, and put it back with the gentleness of a mother tucking a child into bed.

"How's the captain?" Blackie asked.

"Sleeping peacefully. Were you aware of the captain's sympathies?"

Blackie offered him a small smile. "My captain fancies himself a rebel."

"And from your accent, I assume you are not?"

Blackie's smile grew. "Accent? I do not have an accent." His pleasant expression slowly faded. "We have a bit of a problem. Come. There is something I must show you." Blackie headed to the door.

Lorenzo scrambled to the top deck behind him. A strong wind slapped him in the face and set the schooner flying over the waves. Wisps of hair blew into Lorenzo's eyes.

Sailors were busy cleaning the mess that the storm had left on deck, mopping up water, checking the sails for rips.

The sky remained overcast, hiding the sun behind a cloud-bank, but the storm was over, and they had survived.

Legs astraddle, hands clasped behind his back, Blackie nodded at the great empty sea that stretched for mile after mile. As usual, his face revealed no emotion. "I regret this unfortunate development, Dr. Bannister."

"Where is the San Juan Nepomuceno?" Lorenzo asked.

"I haven't a clue," Blackie replied.

Chapter Eight

A thousand questions filled Lorenzo's mind as he scanned the sea for the missing ship. Blackie stood at his side on the quarterdeck.

"Not to worry," Blackie said. "She did not sink."

"What makes you think that?"

"She's much larger than we and less likely to have been swamped during the storm. When it hit, we were far from shore, so chances are she did not wreck. She's out there." Blackie paused. "Somewhere."

"How will you find her?"

"The odds of crossing paths with her are enormous. The best thing to do is to head for New Orleans. It was our original destination before the captain fell ill."

"How long will it take to get to Louisiana?"

"I don't know."

"Where are we?"

"I don't know."

"What do you know?"

Blackie half-turned to him. "We are in the Gulf of Mexico."

"That's it? That's all you know?"

"Mr. Crowe is the navigator, not I. It was most unhelpful of your captain to take him hostage."

"You must have navigational instruments onboard. A compass? A sextant?"

"Not versed in the nautical arts, are we?"

"Am I wearing a navy uniform?" Lorenzo shot back.

"A sextant measures the height of the sun or other heavenly bodies." Blackie spoke in a patient voice as if he were explaining to a little child. "If I know the angle of the sun, I can look on my charts and figure out where I am." He waved his hand at the thick cloud cover. "Until this clears, celestial navigation will do us no good. Now, as to the compass you mentioned, it will help me travel in a straight line. It will not give me a point of reference or tell me where I am. I have no idea how far off course the storm blew us. Until I spot a landmark or God sees fit to remove the cloud cover, our instruments are useless. Understand?"

"Completely."

"Good."

A sailor approached with the jacket Lorenzo had taken off during the operation and held it while Lorenzo slipped into it. He handed him his hat as well and left.

"What will your captain do with my men?" Blackie asked.

"How should I know?"

"Your best guess?"

"I suspect the captain will turn them over to General Gálvez. As governor of Louisiana, he is in charge of all legal and military matters."

"What will General Gálvez do with them?"

"Probably turn them loose. They haven't committed a crime, other than a little piracy."

"Piracy!" Blackie exclaimed indignantly. "We are not pirates. We are privateers."

Lorenzo shrugged. "One man's privateer is another man's pirate."

"We are not pirates!" Blackie repeated.

In a perverse kind of way, Lorenzo enjoyed teasing Blackie. "Whether it's highway robbery or robbery on the high seas, stealing is still stealing."

Blackie studied him through narrow eyes as if trying to read him.

In spite of himself, Lorenzo smiled. "Put your mind at ease. Don Bernardo will not harm your men. He will ask them a few questions and release them."

"How can you be so sure?"

"Because I know him. He has a good heart."

* * *

General Gálvez dipped his quill in ink and bent over a piece of parchment. He wrote a couple of words to his uncle, José De Gálvez, then re-dipped his quill and wrote some more. Searching for just the right phrase, he paused. The first thing that leaped to mind sounded awkward. He twirled around in his chair, rested his boots on the bookcase, and gazed out at New Orleans. His office window offered a view of St. Louis church and the parade ground.

He loved New Orleans, especially in December. The temperature hovered around sixty-five degrees. The sultry days of July and August were past and the dangerous hurricane months had ended in November. He wished he were outside, but being governor meant a perpetual mound of paperwork. Sometimes he felt like Sisyphus condemned for all eternity to roll a boulder up a steep hill.

While thinking about everlasting tasks, the perfect phrase came to him. He whirled around and put quill to parchment. He finished the letter and pulled another piece of paper from his desk drawer.

A rap at the door made him look up.

Lieutenant Sánchez peeped inside. "There's a chap downstairs named Morgan. He's asking to see you, sir, but he doesn't have an appointment."

"David Morgan?"

Lieutenant Sánchez nodded.

"Show him in," Gálvez said, both pleased and surprised by the unexpected visit. He had not seen the boy since Lorenzo's wedding, when he had played the fife. Gálvez put down his quill and stood.

Morgan stepped inside. He was eighteen years old, but looked about fourteen and stood only 5'3".

Gálvez was surprised to see him out of uniform. The last

time they had met, Morgan had been a private in the British army.

Morgan put one hand in front, one behind, and bowed low. "*Bonjour, mon général.*"

"*Monsieur Morgan! C'est un plaisir.*"

"*Pour moi aussi!*"

Gálvez indicated that he was to take a seat. He considered Davy Morgan part of his circle of friends and would forever be grateful for the kindness he had shown Eugenie when she was ill with scarlet fever. He had befriended her, not knowing Gálvez considered her an adopted daughter.

Morgan eased into an armchair and crossed his legs, seemingly more at ease than the last time Gálvez had talked to him. Two months earlier, a terrified private in the British army had fidgeted while standing in front of Gálvez's desk and had looked like a man expecting a death sentence. Gálvez had asked him to go into exile to care for Colonel Robert Hawthorne while he recuperated from rheumatic fever. The lad, a prisoner of war, had gladly accepted.

Now, as the general perched on the edge of his desk and smiled down at Morgan, he silently congratulated himself. Exile with a man of Hawthorne's position had been good for the boy. No longer was he a redcoat in a tattered uniform. Today, he wore silk and satin.

"Colonel Hawthorne sent me," Morgan said.

Gálvez smiled. Of course he had. Hawthorne, banished from Spanish territory, had to conduct business through a third party. "How is the good colonel?" Gálvez asked.

"He is still a little weak, but getting stronger by the day."

"Your French has improved," Gálvez said. "Are you still studying it?"

"Yes, sir. Colonel Hawthorne gives me lessons and makes me speak it for two hours a day. If I say a word in English . . ." Morgan's voice trailed as he made a slicing motion across his neck.

Gálvez laughed. French was the language of diplomacy and polite society. With a French wife and stepdaughter, he found it essential. Speaking it also endeared him to the people of New Orleans, where most spoke French.

"Where do you and Colonel Hawthorne live now?"

"Mobile."

"Mobile," Gálvez repeated, giving himself time to absorb that. Hawthorne, a man who had once worked for British intelligence, was a mere hundred miles away. Why? Had he figured out that Mobile was the next target?

"Why didn't Colonel Hawthorne go back to England to recuperate?"

"His wife lives there."

"Is that a problem?"

"They are happiest when there is an ocean between them."

"Ah!" the general said. "What can I do for you, Mr. Morgan?"

"The colonel asked me to go to his house in Baton Rouge and pick up a personal item."

"The colonel's house was confiscated. It now belongs to Major Calderón."

"Oh, yes sir! The colonel knows that. He only wants to get something from the house."

"What?"

"The portrait in the parlor."

A chill went through Gálvez. He had visited Héctor Calderón at his new home and had seen the portrait. It was beyond ghoulish to look into the faces of the former owners, Evan and Josephine Hawthorne, and their two-year-old daughter, Abigail.

Josephine and Abigail were buried in the family plot beside the house. According to their tombstones, they had died on the same day. Héctor had asked around and discovered that they had died of small pox. No one seemed to know what had happened to Evan.

Gálvez picked up a quill. "Legally, everything in the house belongs to Major Calderón," he said as he wrote, "but I will ask him to give you the portrait."

Morgan sat on the edge of his chair and strained to see what the general was writing. "Could you tell him it has deep sentimental value? The man in the portrait is Colonel Hawthorne's brother."

"Yes, I'll add that."

Gálvez had noticed a strong physical resemblance between Hawthorne and the man in the portrait. He finished the note to Héctor and rocked an ink blotter over it. He folded it and sealed it with wax. "Give this to Major Calderón."

"Thank you, General." Morgan stood to go. "By your leave." He bowed.

"I wish you a safe trip."

Morgan headed to the door.

"Mr. Morgan . . ."

He swiveled.

"God go with you." It wasn't what the general wished to say. He wanted to tell Morgan to get out of Mobile, but he could not do that without tipping his hand. Gálvez had shelled the devil out of Morgan and Hawthorne at Baton Rouge. He did not relish doing so again, but there was no way to warn them that they would soon be in a battle zone.

Chapter Nine

Lorenzo moved to the window in the captain's cabin and peeled back the dressing over his middle finger. He examined the cut. It was not very deep and did not need stitches, but would leave a small scar. What a shame Eugenie wasn't here. Her medical treatment would have been to kiss it to make it feel better.

A sailor appeared in the doorway, leaning on Abercrombie's shoulder. He took a step and grimaced in pain.

Lorenzo leaped from his chair. "What's the problem?"

"Small accident, sir. Got hit in the knee."

The injured man peeped inside the captain's cabin with an expression that suggested he had never seen the inside before. He remained on the threshold.

Not knowing ship's etiquette, Lorenzo decided it was best not to invite the man inside. Medical bag in hand, he went to the cabin door.

"Let me see it," he said.

The man limped to a barrel at the foot of the companionway and dutifully rolled up his pant leg. There was an ugly bruise on his knee. Lorenzo pressed gently against the dark oval and felt a bump. "It's a contusion," Lorenzo said. "It will go away on its own. Stay off it as much as possible." Lorenzo fished around in his medical bag, found a bottle of medicine, and handed it to Abercrombie. "Give your friend a spoonful of this every four hours."

Abercrombie took the painkiller and put it in his pocket.

The injured man reached for the oilskin pouch hanging around his neck. "How much do I owe you?"

Lorenzo waved off the question. "Consider yourself lucky. I'm not charging today."

"Gee, thanks!"

Lorenzo did not realize the enormity of his mistake for a good fifteen minutes. In that length of time, more sailors appeared at his door with maladies ranging from a splinter in the big toe to a sore throat. Before long, there was a line of ten sailors waiting to see him.

Who is sailing the ship? Lorenzo wondered. There were only thirty crewmen in all.

He positioned a chair outside the cabin door at an angle that allowed him to see the captain while treating the crew. Every thirty minutes, Lorenzo checked the captain's pulse and temperature and found them normal. He continued to sleep off the effects of the amputation, but moaned in pain from time to time.

Finally, the last two sailors in line reached Lorenzo.

"Begging the doctor's pardon," one of them said, nervously twirling his sea cap between his hands, "but me mate here's been hurt. Hit on the head by a boom during the storm."

Lorenzo held a candle to the man's eyes to see if they were dilated. Both appeared the same size, a very good sign. "Follow the flame," he said, moving the candle back and forth slowly.

The man complied.

"Where were you hit?"

The man hesitated.

His mate answered, "On the forecastle, sir."

Lorenzo choked back a laugh. "Were you hit on the forehead? The back of the head?"

"There, sir." The pirate pointed vaguely to his forehead.

Lorenzo examined it. If a boom had hit him there, a goose egg should have formed by now. He lightly touched the man's forehead. Sailors, soldiers, or pirates. They all shared one thing. Some of them worked hard at avoiding work.

Lorenzo put on the sternest look he could muster. "That looks bad. Head injuries can be nasty affairs. The best remedy is to return to work and take your mind off it."

"Sir!" the talkative one protested. "He might keel over at any time. Don't you think it be best that he lay down? A mate needs to keep watch to make sure he's all right."

"No, no," Lorenzo said in pretend surprise. "That is the worst thing he could do. Pulling a full four-hour watch is just the thing." Lorenzo put his hand to his mouth as if deep in thought. "Come to think of it, back-to-back watches would be even better. I shall speak to Mr. Blackie at once about that."

"No, no, no!" the talker said, waving his hands dramatically. "I think he feels better already. Ain't that right, Johnny Boy?"

Johnny Boy, apparently the duller of the two, did not immediately catch on.

The talker poked him in the ribs.

"Yeah, yeah. I feel good."

"Are you sure?" Lorenzo said, crouching slightly to peer up at the man. "I'm sure Mr. Blackie would—"

"We best be going," the talkative sailor said, grabbing Johnny Boy by the arm and propelling him up the companionway.

Lorenzo turned and went inside the captain's cabin to keep the sailors from seeing him laugh at them. He found the captain awake and peering at him through half-closed eyes.

"You done good. Them's the laziest two sailors I ever laid eyes on."

"How are you feeling?"

"Good . . . Good."

Lorenzo doubted that, but recalled something that Blackie had said. The captain was not the kind of man to complain, no matter how bad he felt.

Lorenzo sat on the edge of the bunk. He checked the captain's pulse and temperature, then made a notation on the chart Blackie started.

There was a knock on the door.

Lorenzo opened to find Abercrombie holding a tray of food.

"Mr. Blackie told me to bring this to you."

Lorenzo moved out of the way so Abercrombie could put the tray on the table.

The boy whipped off the linen covering to reveal a teapot and two plates with boiled lobster and peas. "Compliments of Mr. Blackie," Abercrombie said.

"Don't know what I'd do without Blackie," the captain said. "Best thing I ever did was bring him aboard."

Abercrombie propped up the captain with pillows, placed a tray in front of him, poured a cup of tea and handed it to him.

The captain took a sip. "Brewed to perfection, as always."

Beaming with delight, Abercrombie replied, "Thank you, Captain." He placed a plate on the tray. "Dr. Bannister," he said, nodding toward the table. "That plate is for you."

Lorenzo sat at the table, thinking: *Pirates dine on lobster. Sure. Why not? Seafood is all around us.* Somehow, he had a mental image of pirates eating lesser fare, maybe sea biscuits washed down with rum.

The captain ate a bite and washed it down with tea. He closed his eyes a moment before taking another bite. Lorenzo could tell he was in pain and could barely eat but was too proud to complain.

Watching a one-armed man feed himself made Lorenzo feel awkward and useless. He wanted to help him, but restrained himself. The captain did fine without him.

"Will you be needing anything else, Captain?" Abercrombie asked.

"Does Cookie have anything for dessert?"

Lorenzo caught Abercrombie's eye and shook his head furiously.

The boy looked perplexed.

Lorenzo stood and walked over to the bunk. "Captain, we need to discuss your diet. Certain items are now forbidden to you."

The captain peeped around Lorenzo and spoke to Abercrombie. "I want dessert as usual."

Lorenzo frowned down at the captain. "The captain will get no more desserts. From now on, there is no sugar in his diet. He will take his tea with lemon and nothing else. I'll discuss the captain's new diet in detail later."

"Blast you!" the captain said. "You don't rule here."

"In medical matters, I outrank you."

"I want you off my ship."

"I'm sure you do, sir, but while I am aboard, you will follow my orders." Lorenzo turned toward Abercrombie. "No more desserts."

White as a sail, Abercrombie took Lorenzo's last statement as an excuse to bolt away.

Lorenzo felt sorry for him. It must have been difficult to be caught between the captain's wishes and his health.

"Blast it all," the captain mumbled. "This is Blackie's fault."

"Moments ago, you were praising the wisdom of bringing him aboard," Lorenzo pointed out.

He wanted to pump the captain for information about

the Englishman, but did not want to be obvious about it. He had not been able to place Blackie, although he sensed he knew him. His British accent made Lorenzo search through memories of serving in the Continental Army. He pictured Blackie as a redcoat and tried to figure out where they had crossed paths.

"Blackie was by your side throughout the operation," Lorenzo said. "In fact, he was quite helpful. I had a minor accident during surgery and Blackie took over."

"He did?" The captain's face reflected deep interest.

"He finished the operation for me. Blackie is talented in the medical arts. Why isn't he practicing medicine?"

The captain chewed slowly. His eyes held a faraway look. "Are you telling me Blackie knows enough medicine to be a doctor?"

"Yes. He was faced with two medical emergencies—my finger and your sutures. He did not have to think twice. It came naturally to him."

"Blackie is a doctor," the captain muttered.

"Apparently, this is news to you," Lorenzo said.

The captain nodded. "It's news to Blackie, too."

"What?" Lorenzo asked, startled by the remark.

"Bring your plate over here, Doc. We need to talk."

Balancing the plate in one hand, a cup of tea in the other, he moved to a chair by the captain's bunk. "How is it possible for Blackie not to know he's a doctor?" Lorenzo asked, setting his cup on the floor.

"He can't remember anything about his past," the captain said. "He doesn't know where he came from or what his name is."

"You can't be serious!" Lorenzo said. He ate several bites of food before the captain responded.

"Let me tell you about Blackie. I think you'll find his story interesting." He paused and seemed to gather his thoughts. "First time I saw him was about eight months ago. I had gone to Fort Charlotte on business. You know where that is?"

"I've heard of it."

Heard of it? Lorenzo and General Gálvez had poured over maps and drawings of the fort looking for the best method of attack. Lorenzo had memorized every square inch of Fort Charlotte and the surrounding town of Mobile.

"I stopped at a tavern on the outskirts of Mobile," the captain said, "and saw Blackie in the stable. He didn't see me. He was singing a hymn and taking care of his horse. It was all black. Bad luck, black horses. Anyway, he was giving it grain. Man's character comes out in two ways—in the way he treats animals and the way he acts when he thinks no one is watching. Have you ever seen a tortured soul, Doc?"

Lorenzo nodded. "Blackie was a tortured soul?" he guessed.

"Devil had his pitchfork in the man and was twisting the handle. I went inside the tavern. Saw Blackie come in a little later. Invited him to break bread with me. When I asked his name, he hesitated. There was a strange, confused look on his face, like that was the first time he realized he didn't know it."

"How curious," Lorenzo said.

"Indeed. I wondered how that was possible. I've seen men conked in the head and out of it for a little while, but I had never seen anyone who genuinely did not know his name."

"Did you ever find it out?"

"No. I started calling him Blackie because he dressed all in black like a doctor. I joked about him being a sawbones. Didn't know I had hit the nail on the head. He's a good man who has been through something terrible. The mind is a marvel. If something is too painful, it will shut down and block a memory until the person is able to accept or understand."

Lorenzo nodded. He had been in battle. He remembered charging into chaos, death and destruction, only vaguely aware of who was at his side, what was going on around him. Some men claimed vivid memories of every second of battle. Not Lorenzo. His mind became as smoky as the battlefield. When everything was over, he was himself again. His mind had blocked out painful experiences.

"You've been through something yourself," the captain stated.

Lorenzo jerked his head up, surprised by the man's foresight.

The captain smiled sadly. "When you get to be my age, you see things in people's faces."

"So Blackie was a waif you took aboard your ship?"

"A well-educated waif. Gives himself away by the fancy words he uses. They roll off his tongue natural-like. I've figured out a few things about him. I know he's British, a Methodist, well educated."

"Married," Lorenzo added.

The captain cocked his head. "How do you figure that? He doesn't wear a wedding ring."

"He used to. It left an indentation. I've only been married two months but the ring has already left its mark. The skin beneath it is untanned."

"Blackie is married," the captain said.

"Or was. After all, he took the ring off."

The captain chewed on that bit of information.

Blackie burst into the room. He dashed to the drawer beneath the captain's bed, yanked it open, and rooted around in it.

"Speak of the devil," the captain said, "and he shall appear."

Lorenzo noticed that Blackie paid no attention to the remark and failed to greet them. It was uncharacteristically rude behavior.

He opened a big box.

The captain looked alarmed. "What are you doing?"

"Ship's on the horizon." Blackie took out an enormous Union Jack. "A British frigate."

Chapter Ten

C an you outrun her?" the captain asked.

"I shall do my best, sir," Blackie answered. "I want to have this handy in case I need to run it up."

"Wise move," the captain said.

Blackie acknowledged Lorenzo with a nod. "Sorry to interrupt your dinner." He bolted out the door.

"May I ask a question, Captain?" Lorenzo asked.

"Fire away."

"Why is Blackie going to fly a British flag?"

The captain leaned deep into his pillows. "It's called flying false colors. Because we are at war, international law lets us trick the enemy. We can fly another country's flag and make them think we are neutral or a ship of their own navy. If we had enough cannons, we could get close enough to the frigate to blow her out of the water. But we don't, so the best policy is to run like the devil. Listen, I'm fine as a fiddle. Go topside and tell me what's afoot."

By the time Lorenzo stepped on deck, Blackie had already hoisted the Union Jack and had the sails all full. His deep voice rang over the deck, spitting out orders. Sailors went about their various tasks, faces dark with concentration. The Liberty traveled at top speed.

The ship chasing them was quite a distance to the rear. Lorenzo could barely make out the British flag. He wondered about the name of the ship, but seeing it from this angle made it impossible to see anything but the bow. That meant the British ship had a view of the Liberty's stern and could see the name spelled out in bold letters.

For several minutes, Lorenzo watched the chase. The other ship fell farther and farther behind. Finally, she gave up completely and turned away.

A cheer went up from the crew. An impromptu celebration broke out. Someone started to play a merry tune on a mouth organ. Pirates began to dance a jig around the forecastle.

Joy flooded Lorenzo as well. He liked to dance and he found himself wanting to join in the celebration. The deck before the mast was not officer country, so he remained on the quarterdeck, watching and tapping his foot to the music.

Blackie joined him, grinning like a madman.

"Good work," Lorenzo said.

Blackie ignored the compliment. "Do not say a word to the captain about that." He nodded to the dancing sailors. "He would have a conniption if he knew there was dancing on his ship."

"Why?" Lorenzo asked.

"Captain's a Baptist and—"

"Let me guess. They don't believe in dancing."

Blackie aimed a finger at him. "No dancing. No card playing. No liquor."

"*Madre de Dios*," Lorenzo mumbled. "What do they do for fun?"

Blackie seemed to understand that the question expected no answer.

"Land ho!" the lookout called, pointing toward the west where the sun balanced half in and half out of the sea.

Lorenzo squinted at a tiny dot in the distance while Blackie used a spyglass to scan it.

He gave Lorenzo a wicked look. "I have good news. I finally know where we are."

"About time."

Blackie tugged on his shirtfront as if offended by the comment. "I shall ignore your cheap jibe, Lorenzo."

Lorenzo turned to him. "Are we now on a first-name basis? I thought you English believed in good manners and etiquette."

"Have I offended you?"

"When you offend me, you'll know. I'll call you out for a duel."

Blackie snorted at him. "If I'm not mistaken—and I so rarely am—that is Isla Mujeres. That means we are off the coast of the Yucatan. If we sail into a Spanish-speaking port, we will need a translator."

"I charge for my services."

Blackie smiled. "That's not what I hear from my sailors. They said you gave them free medical services."

A sudden thought struck Lorenzo. "If you sail into Spanish waters, which flag will you fly?"

"Not the Union Jack. Spain and Great Britain are at war. That leaves either American or French. If you had rooted around a bit more in the drawer, you would have discovered a French flag as well as the Union Jack. Unfortunately, we don't have a Spanish one. Be a good fellow and get one for us at the earliest opportunity."

"So you can get close to a Spanish ship and blow it out of the water?"

"We would never do that!"

"Because you don't have enough fire power?"

"I wouldn't say that." Blackie called to the boatswain, "I am going below to visit the captain."

"Aye, sir," the man replied.

Lorenzo stayed on the top deck to give Blackie and the captain some privacy. Twilight over the island deepened and the stars came out. He thought about Eugenie. Was she looking at the same stars?

On their last night together before he went to Cuba, both of them were restless. They knew how dangerous the military was, but never discussed it. Eugenie still bore a small scar on her forehead as the result of an unfortunate encounter with red-coats. Lorenzo had a star-shaped scar from the time Saber-Scar had shot him in the back.

"I can't sleep," Lorenzo had whispered.

"Me neither," Eugenie replied. "I'm famished. Want to go downstairs and get something to eat?"

"Sure." Lorenzo wondered how she could be hungry. She had eaten a hearty meal at dinner, served in the Spanish fashion at eight o'clock.

After throwing on robes and lighting candles to guide their way, they visited Don Bernardo's larder. Eugenie prepared a platter of cheese, pickles, olives, sliced ham, boiled eggs, rolls, and a flask of water while Lorenzo watched in dismay.

"Are we going to eat all that?" he asked.

"We? Were you planning to eat some of this?"

"*Dios mío*, Eugenie. Can you eat all that yourself?"

"I'm hungry."

"If you keep eating like this, I'm going to have to roll you out the door."

"What will you do if I get fat? Other than roll me out the door?"

Lorenzo chuckled. "I'll love you no matter how fat you get."

"Good answer. I like a man who thinks fast on his feet."

They slipped into the courtyard where they sat at the patio table and ate. They whispered and laughed and watched the moon sail across the starry sky.

When the tray was half gone, they heard the door leading to the patio open and close.

Don Bernardo edged toward them in the moon-bright courtyard, pistol at the ready. He stopped ten feet short of the patio table. "Forever more!" he exclaimed. "What are you two doing up at this hour?"

"Emptying your larder," Eugenie said.

"That's a good way to get shot," he grumbled. "Felicité woke me from a sound sleep because of you two. She said she heard robbers in the courtyard."

Lorenzo could not help but laugh. Eugenie smiled and shook her head.

Grumbling about youth being wasted on the young, Don Bernardo had given Eugenie a kiss on the cheek and had gone back inside.

The memory comforted Lorenzo. Eugenie would always have a home with Don Bernardo and Doña Felicité, should she need one.

* * *

Blackie sat at the captain's bedside and told him about outrunning the British frigate.

"Good work," the captain said in a feeble voice. "I fear they know about the chest and are looking for it."

Blackie nodded.

"At all cost," the captain said, "we must keep it out of British hands. Bury it on Isla Mujeres. We can come back for it when the danger has passed."

"Aye, Captain."

"Take the letter of marque. Keep it on you. With the British skulking about, I would feel better knowing you have it at hand."

Blackie went to the drawer beneath the captain's bed, took out the letter, folded it, and stashed it in his oilskin pouch.

"If capture is unavoidable," the captain said, "your first task is to get Bannister off the ship and destroy all evidence he was ever here. The British have not forgotten that the Spaniards defeated them at Baton Rouge. A Spanish officer is a complication you do not need."

"What will they do if they find him onboard?"

"Hang him. After that, they will be less inclined to show my sailors mercy. One more thing. Promise me that you will sink the Liberty before you let it fall into British hands. I don't want her to become a prize."

"Sir, I can't do that!"

"Of course, you can! If there is no way to avoid capture, run up the American flag. That will give you and all the others onboard prisoner-of-war status. Order the men to abandon ship, go to the powder magazine, and blow her up."

Blackie ran his hands through his hair.

"Promise me," the captain ordered.

It will never happen, Blackie told himself. I outran the enemy once. I can do it again. "I promise," Blackie said, to put the captain's mind at ease.

Looking relieved, the captain closed his eyes and fell asleep.

* * *

Blackie came from below decks with two young pirates lugging a chest. It looked like the one Lorenzo had seen in the captain's room.

The ship dropped anchor. Sailors readied the longboat and put the chest in the middle of the boat. Blackie and ten crewmen, all with knives and pistols in their belts and some with shovels, set out for shore. A sailor sat in the bow and held a lantern over the water to spot danger. Cones of light danced across the waves.

Lorenzo watched pirates reach the shore, tie the boat, and carry the chest behind the trees. Fifteen minutes later, they returned without it.

Lorenzo went to the captain's cabin. Sure enough, the chest was missing.

He removed his jacket and hung it on a peg. He plopped into a chair by the bunk where the captain was dozing and took Dr. Buchan's *Domestic Medicine* from his bag. He plumped some pillows, arranged them in the chair, nestled a blanket around himself, and settled in for a long read. The medical text, published in 1769, covered everything: pleurisy, small pox inoculation, whooping cough, worms, jaundice, dropsy, gout, pregnancy, childbirth, and teething. Lorenzo thought he had found what he was looking for when he reached a chapter on nervous diseases. He scanned it and found melancholy, the palsy, epilepsy, nightmares—even hiccups. Nothing fit Blackie's condition.

It was a puzzle to be solved, and Lorenzo was determined to find the answer. Had any of his father's patients had a similar problem? Not that he could remember.

The sun set. Lorenzo looked out at the darkening sky and thought about everything that had happened.

My first day on a pirate ship, he said to himself, I amputated a leg, outran a British frigate, and watched pirates bury treasure on a deserted island. I treated a number of patients for free. What was I thinking? And I met a pirate with a mental disorder.

All in all, a good day's work.

Chapter Eleven

Lorenzo awoke to the sound of men running about on the deck overhead. Voices shouted orders. Other voices answered them.

"Weigh anchor!" That was Blackie. A sudden urgency replaced his normal calm.

It took Lorenzo a moment to shake off sleep and realize he had spent the night in a chair next to the captain's bunk.

Early morning sunlight crept into the room. Today is December 16, 1779, Lorenzo thought. The book he had been reading lay on the floor. He picked it up and put in back in his medical bag. After a quick check of the patient, Lorenzo reached for his jacket, but changed his mind. As long as he was stuck on a pirate ship, he might as well be comfortable. He headed upstairs to see what was going on.

Ten sailors turned the capstan, a giant winch that pulled up the anchor. It looked like an oversized wagon wheel on its side. Sailors stood inside the spokes and pushed on them with all their might, walking in a circle. The capstan reeled in a massive iron chain attached to the anchor. Others were in the rigging unfurling sails. Blackie stood on the quarterdeck where he could see everything.

Lorenzo felt fear in the air. He scanned the horizon and saw two British warships side by side on the northern horizon. Suddenly, they split off in two directions, and Lorenzo instinctively knew what they were doing. One of them would attack from the east while the other would maneuver behind the schooner. A shot to the stern would send a cannonball straight through to the powder magazine. To deliver a broadside, they had to sail parallel to her, either on the left or right. A couple of well-placed cannonballs would cripple the ship or sink her.

The schooner had anchored for the night on the northern point of Isla Mujeres. The island lay to the right. With enemy ships bearing down on them, the schooner had no option but to sail south. She took off dreadfully slow, but as wind filled the sails, she picked up speed. Soon, she was flying before the enemy. Isla Mujeres disappeared behind her.

The British warships moved at an impressive speed, but the Liberty was faster, always staying a step ahead of the bow guns.

She kept the rising sun to the left. As usual, Blackie stood on the quarterdeck with his legs slightly apart, hands laced behind him, his face showing no emotion. It was a stance that said, "I am master of this ship and no one need worry while I am at the helm."

In the short time he had been onboard, Lorenzo had noticed something odd about the way the sailors treated Blackie. They had a variety of names for him, from "The Ace of Spades" to "Mister B," but they never spoke in a scornful tone and never used nicknames in his presence.

He was a natural leader, not one who had to use fear to have his orders obeyed. Lorenzo suspected he had once been in the military, the Royal Navy, perhaps.

The Liberty's lead stretched and the threat from the two ships shrank. Everyone onboard seemed to sag in relief.

Thinking that all the excitement was over, Lorenzo went below. The captain was sleeping. That was understandable, considering what his body had been through. Sometimes sleep was the best medicine. Lorenzo unwrapped the captain's leg to examine it. The gangrene seemed to have been checked. He put a new dressing on it.

By the time he returned to the main deck, the two ships were so far back, they were hard to see—but they were still in pursuit.

Lorenzo walked up to Blackie. "I see we still have our escort."

"They insist upon following us. For some small and trivial reason, I find that quite vexing."

"What do you intend to do about them?"

"Run until the hounds grow tired and abandon the chase."

"Why are they chasing us?"

Blackie smiled. "The British are an odd lot."

"They're putting a lot of effort into this."

"Yes, I know."

Was there something onboard that they were after? Or someone? Blackie, perhaps?

Lorenzo cleared his throat. "I would like to point something out. We are heading in the wrong direction. New Orleans is that way." He pointed over his shoulder.

"Not to worry. I promised to deliver you safe and sound. I am a man of my word."

A piece of land came into view. It turned out to be an island far bigger than the one they had left.

"Welcome to Cozumel," Blackie said.

Lorenzo liked the sound of the name. He spotted a dilapidated stone building. "Who lives on the island?"

"No one. It has been deserted for as long as anyone can remember."

It seemed a pity. In all his travels, Lorenzo had never seen anything that so closely resembled paradise. Palm trees swayed in the breeze. Blindingly white beaches merged with a turquoise sea. Fish flitted about in crystal-clear water. Dolphins leaped beside the ship.

As they cruised along the eastern coastline, Blackie ordered some of the sails furled. He caught Lorenzo's questioning look and half-smiled. "I intend to circle the island and want the ships to follow us. I should very much like to keep them in the line of sight so I know where they are at all times. There are several reefs on the west side. With any luck, our friends will crash into one. Come. I'll show you." He went to the chart table, where an unrolled map was held down by weights. "When we get here," he said, pointing to the waters off the southernmost tip of the island, "we pick up a south-north current. It should help us on our way."

They followed the coast, rounded the cape and turned north.

Blackie looked aft. The two ships had gained a little ground, but were still too far behind to be a threat. He ordered the boatswain to unfurl all sails.

They came thundering down. Wind filled the sails and the Liberty picked up speed.

Blackie placed his fingertips against his forehead in a mock salute to the British ships. "Adieu, mes copains. Vive le roi."

Blackie's French was flawless. Lorenzo made a mental note of that. It wasn't Eugenie's French Canadian dialect or the creole of Felicité de Gálvez. It reminded him of the kind of French the Marquis de la Fayette spoke.

Lorenzo tracked the schooner's progress on the map. The western coast was the most rugged section with a number of coves and reefs. The Liberty headed north. It approached the place where the island narrowed and tapered to a point.

On the eastern side of the island, a bit of material at the top of a pole grabbed Lorenzo's attention. It moved parallel to them. It took a moment to realize what he was seeing—a pennant at the top of a mast. He drew in a long breath of surprise.

"No!" Blackie exclaimed, shock on his face.

In unison, Lorenzo and Blackie swiveled. The two ships

were still behind them.

"Ship to starboard!" the lookout called.

A bowsprit and sails glided into view, followed by a wooden carving of King Neptune. The rest of the ship emerged from behind the island. It was the British frigate that had chased them the previous evening.

Chapter Twelve

Blackie ordered the Liberty to turn hard to port, but it was too late.

The ship was closing on them. Lorenzo could see sailors on the deck and in the rigging. It had thirty guns, twelve on each side, two on the quarterdeck, two on the stern, and two on the bow.

Abercrombie came on deck, rubbing sleep from his eyes. "What the hell is going on?" He directed the question to the first person he met, which happened to be Lorenzo. "Pardon my French, sir. What perchance is afoot?"

Instead of answering, Lorenzo pointed to the British ship.

"Oh, dear Lord!" Abercrombie exclaimed.

"Abercrombie," Blackie yelled, "go below and get the Stars and Stripes."

The boy dashed away.

At that instant, the frigate fired a salvo from the bow guns. Two balls screamed through the Liberty's mainsail and shrouds, narrowly missing the mast.

"Man the cannons!" Blackie yelled.

Pirates scrambled to the two cannons on the right side of the ship. They primed and loaded them.

"Fire when ready!" Blackie bellowed.

The boatswain sighted one of them, put a linstock to the touchhole, and ignited the charge.

The shot hit one of the longboats on the enemy's main deck and turned it into kindling.

Johnny Boy and his talkative friend manned the second cannon. They fired, but the shot fell short and sent up a spray of water twenty feet from the enemy ship.

"Lower Number One!" Blackie ordered. "Number Two, aim for the waterline."

Lorenzo slipped over to Blackie who was pacing back and forth from cannon to cannon. "May I help?"

Blackie looked surprised by the offer. "Do you know how to fire a cannon?"

Lorenzo nodded. He had learned at the Battle of Baton Rouge.

"Man that one," Blackie said, gesturing to Johnny Boy's cannon.

Under Lorenzo's direction, Johnny Boy and his friend set about reloading and repositioning the cannon, an operation that took two minutes. Lorenzo sighted it.

In the meantime, Abercrombie returned with the American flag and handed it to Blackie who hoisted it up.

"Fire!" Lorenzo ordered.

The cannonball nicked the frigate's figurehead. Lorenzo had been aiming for the swivel cannon on the bow. "*Madre de Dios,*" he mumbled. The last time he fired a cannon, the target, Fort Richmond, had not bounced on the waves. Hitting a moving target was harder than it appeared.

In response, the enemy launched a ragged salvo. Lorenzo saw a blast of smoke and a spit of fire from the cannons.

Abercrombie dashed over to Lorenzo's cannon. "Can I—"

Enemy guns blazed again, drowning out the rest of his remark. Shots whizzed overhead, but did little damage.

"That wasn't even close," Lorenzo remarked.

"That's 'cause she's trying to disable us," Abercrombie explained, "not sink us."

"How can you be sure?"

"No profit in it. If we have something valuable onboard, they don't want to put it at the bottom of the sea. You fire a broadside at the waterline if you want to sink a ship."

An instant later, the whining shriek of incoming cannonballs passed overhead. One of them crashed into the longboat. Another blew apart the railing in the deck amidships. Yet another smacked into the main mast.

Sails and rigging rained down forcing everyone to duck, cover their heads, and dodge falling debris.

The main mast looked like a tree struck by lightning. The top portion was reduced to jagged, splintered wood. Some sails were torn. Others were entirely shot away. The rigging was in tatters. Shock froze every man. All sound died.

"Surrender or we will sink you," a voice shouted from the British ship.

"Return the compliment, lads!" Blackie yelled. "Sink her!"

Lorenzo sighted the cannon for the waterline. He stepped to the left and ordered, "Fire!"

The cannonball put a hole in the ship's hull.

Blackie rushed over to Lorenzo's cannon. "Good work! That buys us a little time. They'll have to plug that hole before the ship takes on too much water."

There was a long pause in the shelling. A volley burst from the frigate.

Lorenzo and everyone around him hunkered down.

This time, there was no whining shriek of an incoming cannonball. A swishing sound followed by hard thuds passed overhead. Two sailors hit the deck, one with a hole in the chest, the other with a hole in the forehead.

"Grapeshot," Blackie said in disgust. "They are truly beginning to annoy me."

Lorenzo cast him a questioning look.

"You fire solid cannonballs if you want to disable an enemy ship," Blackie explained. "You fire grapeshot if you want to kill the crew. They can see the damage done to the main mast. They know we can no longer maneuver the ship."

For the first time, Lorenzo understood why Gálvez had used solid cannonballs at the Battle of Baton Rouge. He only wanted to batter Fort Richmond and force a surrender, not slaughter everyone inside it.

The frigate guns roared again. More grapeshot swished across the deck.

Three men crumpled. Lorenzo slid over to them but found them dead. They were the sailors at the amputation.

"Surrender!" a British voice roared from the enemy ship. "Or we will kill every man."

They held their fire, apparently to let Blackie mull over their offer.

"It is only a matter of time before they send a boarding party," Blackie said to Lorenzo. "We have to get you off the ship."

"Me? Why me? What about you and your men?"

"The defeat at Baton Rouge is a recent sore. If they find a Spanish officer onboard, they will vent their rage on you and us. We sail under a letter of marque issued by Congress. If captured, we become prisoners of war."

"When they hear your accent, they will execute you for treason."

"As a privateer, I am entitled to become an honorable prisoner, no matter my nationality."

"In theory," Lorenzo pointed out.

"Always a little ray of sunshine, aren't we?" Blackie forced a smile. "We must get you off the ship now. Can you swim?"

"Yes."

"Can you make it to Cozumel?"

Lorenzo peered in that direction. It did not look very far, but distances could be deceiving. "Yes," he said with more conviction than he felt.

"Where is your uniform?"

"In the captain's cabin."

Hunched over, Blackie headed for the companionway. He disappeared down it with Lorenzo on his heels. He dashed into the captain's cabin and snatched Lorenzo's hat from the table and his jacket from the peg.

"What's going on?" the captain asked.

"Bad news, sir," Blackie replied. "A British frigate has disabled us."

"Blast it all!" The captain chewed his lower lip. "You know what to do."

"Sir—"

"I expect every man to do his duty," the captain said, "including you. Honor your promise."

Blackie ran his hands through his hair in desperation. "But, sir, I cannot in good conscience—"

"The Brits won't wait forever," the captain said gruffly. "You know what to do. Hand me my Bible and get out of here."

Bending over the captain, Blackie kissed him on the forehead. "God bless you, sir. May angels carry you to your rest." He put the requested book in the captain's hands.

Lorenzo observed the exchange in silence. Evidently, the two of them had discussed the action to be taken when capture was inevitable. It looked like the captain planned to go down with his ship.

In a voice devoid of emotion, Blackie said to Lorenzo, "Bring your medical bags."

Lorenzo paused by the captain. "It was an honor to meet you, sir."

"Godspeed, young man."

In the galley, Blackie threw Lorenzo's jacket and hat into the flames. As he stirred the fire with a poker, he asked, "Is there anything in your medical bags that identifies you as a Spanish officer?"

"No, I don't think so."

"But you're not sure."

Lorenzo riffled through the contents. Nothing gave him away except Dr. Buchan's medical book, a gift from Eugenie. On the bookplate, she had written, *Á Lorenzo, mon petit choux. Avec tout mon amour. Eugenie. Baton Rouge, le 12 octobre 1779.*

Blackie peeped over his shoulder. "That has to go into the fire. You cannot leave anything behind."

He did not want to give it up and tried to think of a way to save it. Blackie was right. It had to go. With deep sorrow, Lorenzo fed it to the fire and watched the pages turn to ash.

Blackie headed topside. He passed a series of pegs with burlap bags hanging from them and grabbed one. Lorenzo, carrying his father's medical bags, went with him to the side of the ship facing away from the frigate.

"Take off your boots. They will sink you like an armful of lead."

Lorenzo yanked them off.

Blackie put them inside the bag. He tied the top with twine.

93

"When you reach Cozumel, you will need these. Do everything in your power to grab this bag after you jump into the sea. You can't jump with your medical bags. Leave them here."

Lorenzo hesitated. They had great sentimental value, especially the one that had belonged to his father.

"Hurry," Blackie urged, his gaze going to the frigate.

The frigate lowered one of its remaining longboats.

"Hurry!" Blackie repeated, his voice tinged with anxiety. "They are on their way."

Lorenzo put his medical bags on deck.

"Take this." Blackie handed him a long knife that Lorenzo stuck in his belt. "Cross your arms over your chest before you jump. Keep your legs together, toes pointed down. When you are under the water, fan your arms and legs to propel you to the surface. Into the drink, Lorenzo!"

Lorenzo peeped over the edge of the ship. It was a long way down. He traced a quick cross over his chest.

"Need a push?" Blackie whispered.

Before he could answer, he felt a hard shove from behind. He barely had time to do as Blackie said.

Terror zipped through Lorenzo as he plunged down toward the water. Just before he hit, he closed his eyes, took a deep breath, and held it.

The water was like a slap in the face. It filled his ears. He sank down, down, down. It felt like his lungs would burst. Blackie's words rang in his ears. *Fan your arms and legs.* Lorenzo opened his eyes and looked up. The sea glittered overhead. He struggled toward the light. After what seemed an eternity, he broke the surface. His lungs burned from the effort, as if someone had poured acid into them. Salt water made the wound on his finger sting. He gulped in air and searched for the burlap bag. It floated on top of the water. Lorenzo swam to it and wondered what Blackie had put inside to make it buoyant. He looped the twine handle around his wrist.

Once he had his bearings, he began to swim toward Cozumel.

Excitement made his heart race. He forced himself to calm down and think only of swimming. Panicking was the worst thing he could do. One stroke, two stroke. Turn your head and breathe. One stroke, two stroke. Turn your head and breathe. To save his strength, he changed to a frog kick. It seemed to get him just as far with less effort. Blackie had said there was a strong south-north current. Lorenzo was beginning to understand how much that would drain his strength.

Chapter Thirteen

Robert Hawthorne walked the streets of Mobile clutching a letter edged in black. It had first gone to Philadelphia, where he once worked for British Intelligence, and had followed him to the house he inherited in Baton Rouge and finally to Mobile.

The letter told him his wife was dead. At age twenty-eight, he was a widower. He wandered aimlessly, regret gnawing at him. It had been an arranged marriage forced on him when he was sixteen. He had never loved her, never been faithful to her. The only good thing to come from the marriage was a daughter named Charlotte.

Hawthorne picked up a rock and skipped it over the Mobile River. Why hadn't the letter been from Evan? He held out a ridiculous hope that his younger brother was still alive and some day would write and explain where he had been. Erratic behavior would have been expected, had Evan been an intelligence officer. But he wasn't. He was a surgeon. And he was keen on writing letters and keeping in touch with family.

Hawthorne rubbed the heel of his hand over his forehead. Deep down, he knew Evan was dead. It would be a comfort to know what had happened to him.

*   *   *

Blackie rubbed the heel of his hand over his forehead. He had promised the captain he would not let the British take the Liberty as a prize. With the longboat destroyed, there was no way to save Captain Slaughter. They both knew he was doomed. Blackie could tell that by his resigned expression when he asked for the Bible.

Blackie ran from deck to deck and shouted "Abandon ship!" at the top of his lungs. He hoped everyone was off the Liberty. In the powder magazine, he prepared a long fuse that he trailed out the door and down the deck. Please God, he silently prayed, let it give me enough time to get off the ship. He looked out a porthole and saw the British getting into a longboat. He took a tinderbox from his pocket, struck a spark, and put it to the fuse. When he saw it sputter and catch, he bolted up the companionway to the empty deck.

The heads of his sailors bobbed in the water as they swam away from the ship.

He jumped and joined them.

Chapter Fourteen

Wave after wave of salt water washed over Lorenzo as he struggled toward shore. With each stroke, the island grew closer and he grew wearier. Swimming with the string to the burlap bag looped around one wrist was awkward at best. He paused to take a rest and judge the distance. The island still seemed a long way off. He looked back at the Liberty. From this angle, he could see the boarding party of British sailors in the longboat. They were about halfway to the schooner. Oddly, he could not see anyone on the Liberty. Had Blackie ordered them to abandon ship? Had they jumped into the water? Lorenzo looked for heads bobbing about, but the waves obscured his view. Perhaps Blackie's pirates were hiding on deck and waiting to ambush the British when they came within range.

In a roar of thunder and a burst of crimson flame, the Liberty exploded.

Startled by the sudden sound, Lorenzo jerked back. Debris

rocketed into the air and rained down, some in small pieces, some in big chunks. A large object splashed into the water a few feet away and floated on the waves. Smoke billowed from the ship.

Lorenzo prayed that no one was hurt by the falling wreckage. Had the frigate fired the coup de grace and caused the explosion? If so, he had not seen it. Why would they do that? Usually, a captured prize was sailed to the closest port, where it was sold to the highest bidder.

Lorenzo set out again. He tried not to breathe when waves came toward him but sometimes he misjudged and sucked water into his nostrils. Sometimes, he had his mouth open at the wrong time. The shock of water going down his throat made him stop and cough it out. He wished he could grab onto something to help him float. Swimming was sapping his strength, and he feared he would never make it to the island.

A piece of flotsam rode the waves about thirty feet away. It seemed large, but Lorenzo could not make out what it was. He debated with himself for a moment, then decided to swim toward it, even though it put him farther from the island. When he reached it, he laughed out loud. It was the wheel from the Liberty and it appeared to be intact. He grabbed onto it, worked to get a good hold, and clung on. He took a much-needed rest.

Slowly, smoke from the Liberty drifted away. Lorenzo's eyes raked the area where it had been. Nothing remained except scattered flotsam. The two British ships that had pursued them around Cozumel caught up with the Liberty and took a position west of the frigate.

Something brushed against Lorenzo's leg. He flinched in surprise and looked down at a school of bright yellow fish swimming past. He blew out a long sigh of relief. It was one of the most beautiful sights he had ever seen.

A fin jutted out of the water to his left. The shark attached to it looked enormous, perhaps eight feet long, and did not seem interested in him. Lorenzo watched in growing terror as it swam about. He slipped the knife from his belt and held it at the ready, hoping he would not have to use it.

Suddenly, the shark approached. It began to circle him, going past very slowly.

Lorenzo had seen a shark up close, but it had been dead. A fisherman had harpooned one swimming in the Mississippi River near New Orleans and had put it on display on the wharf. According to old timers, once in a while a shark became disoriented and swam inland. Lorenzo remembered the extraordinarily sharp teeth and kept an eye on the big brute swimming nearby.

The shark gliding through the water was awe-inspiring. Still, it was unnerving knowing that something wanted to eat you. Lorenzo's first impulse was to swim away from the shark. A little voice told him to stay perfectly still.

Each time Lorenzo lost sight of the shark, he quickly rotated his head, wondering what direction it would come from next.

Without warning, the enormous gray mass barreled toward him at full speed while shaking its head from side to side.

Lorenzo panicked and kicked backwards, away from the shark.

It stopped six feet away and veered off. He is as scared of me as I am of him, Lorenzo thought. He froze, holding his knife tightly to fend off an attack.

The shark returned and swam toward Lorenzo. Go for the eye, he told himself. If he can't see you, he might leave you alone.

With one hand, Lorenzo clung to the wheel and waited. He clutched the knife in the other. It had to be just the right moment. The beast came closer. It made a sudden turn and swam away.

For a full minute, Lorenzo did nothing but watch in disbelief as the creature grew more and more distant.

As quickly as it began, it was over. He looked around for other fins. Finding none, he rested before letting go of the ship's wheel and swimming toward Cozumel.

Crack! Crack! Crack! Lorenzo recognized the distant sound at once. It was musket fire. Who was firing? And at whom?

He paused and rotated toward the three British ships. Sailors in the sails and rigging were shooting into the water.

In a moment of sheer terror, Lorenzo realized what was happening.

The British were murdering Blackie's pirates.

* * *

Blackie swam toward Cozumel. He heard something that sounded like an angry bee whiz past his ear and plop into the water. He did not immediately realize what was happening until he glanced over his shoulder and saw British marines shooting from the rigging. His mind refused to believe that they were shooting defenseless men.

He dove underwater and swam until his breath ran out and he had to surface. He found himself within ten feet of Johnny Boy. The sailor looked terrified and gasped for breath.

"They're shooting at us, Mr. B!" the boy exclaimed.

"Swim to Cozumel," Blackie said. "Swim underwater!"

Blackie dove under the water and swam with Johnny Boy at his side.

The shooting continued to send deadly darts into the water.

Johnny Boy jerked. Blackie glanced toward him and stopped swimming. He knew the young man had been shot. Red foam fanned out around him. Arms spread, he drifted toward the surface.

Blackie started to head toward him, but stopped when a shark, mouth wide open, attacked Johnny Boy.

Unable to hold his breath any longer, Blackie surfaced. Fins were everywhere. Dead bodies floated on the surface, face down in the water. One of them was Johnny Boy's friend. His body shook as if it had suddenly come back to life, then went under the water. A red stain grew where he had been. Blackie dove down again and swam away from the sharks feeding off his sailors.

Chapter Fifteen

S hip's in! Ship's in!"

The words filtered through the open window in Gálvez's second-floor office. He jumped from his chair, dashed to the window, and thrust his head out. "Which ship?" he yelled to anyone in the courtyard who cared to answer. He knew his actions were undignified, but he did not care.

"San Juan Nepomuceno," came the reply from a boy crossing the green.

Lorenzo's ship had finally arrived! Gálvez grabbed his hat and coat from the rack behind the door and bolted from his office, dressing on the fly.

As he dashed past soldiers on guard by the main door, it occurred to him that Eugenie may not have heard the news. "Corporal Castillo," he yelled, "go to my house and tell Mrs. Bannister that the San Juan Nepomuceno is in."

On the wharf, he sidestepped a dead rat and made a mental

note to discuss the growing rodent population with the city council. By the time he reached the ship, it had dropped anchor. Like vultures around a carcass, people waited at the foot of a wooden gangway.

A sailor with his arm in a sling was the first off. Next came four men in irons, each in the custody of a marine.

Mutiny immediately came to mind, but upon closer examination, Gálvez rejected the idea. They did not dress like Spanish sailors. The Havana-to-New Orleans route went straight through the Gulf of Mexico and did not pass any islands. Where had these men come from?

Three of the prisoners appeared to be between the ages of sixteen and twenty. They gaped in wide-eyed amazement, evidently admiring New Orleans. One of them nudged a fellow prisoner and nodded toward St. Louis church.

The fourth prisoner wore his beard in braids and looked around as if seeking an escape route. Gálvez took an instant, irrational dislike to him. He was a good judge of character and thought that this fellow's soul was as black as his beard.

The marines marched the prisoners away. Gálvez would visit the jail later, learn the story of their capture, and dispose of them. For now, talking to Lorenzo was of paramount importance.

What was the Captain General's reply to the request for ships and troops? Gleaning information about the latest sea conditions was a priority as well. A hurricane had sunk his ships before the attack on Baton Rouge. The last thing he needed was another storm delaying his attack on Mobile.

Standing still and waiting was torture. To pass the time, Gálvez observed the people of New Orleans. Servants from local inns and taverns flitted about on the wharf and passed out fliers to drum up business. Dockside, merchants supervised the unloading of wares and checked cargo to make sure items had arrived safely. One of those merchants was his best friend, an Irishman named Oliver Pollock, who stood tapping his cane on the ground in eager anticipation. He was talking to Thomas Hancock, the courier between New Orleans and Baton Rouge. No doubt, Thomas was waiting for the bag containing letters bound for points along the river road. The boy was growing into a fine young man.

New Orleans was bursting with new faces, and Gálvez prided himself on knowing the name and situation of each resident. Just then, he noticed Ensign Juan Antonio de Riaño y Bárcena strolling arm-in-arm with Victoria de Saint Maxent, Felicité's sixteen-year-old sister. Trailing behind them was a chaperon, keeping them in sight but giving them breathing room to talk without being overheard.

Gálvez chuckled. Ensign Riaño was an energetic young man who, like so many of his brother officers, had fallen for the charms of a New Orleans beauty. He would make a good husband for Victoria. Better yet, he would make a loyal, trustworthy brother-in-law. Gálvez could tell he was destined for greatness and planned to shepherd him to bigger and better things, just as he planned to help others in his family circle. That included Lorenzo and Eugenie.

The next person to catch his eye was a young sailor with a monkey on his shoulder. He paced back and forth on deck, pausing once in a while to search the crowds. He looked about, not the way a sailor studies a new port, but in a searching kind of way. The monkey wore a collar with a chain and stuffed bits of food in his mouth as quickly as the boy handed them to him.

Gálvez grew tired of waiting and boarded the ship. On his way up the gangway, sailors stiffened and flattened themselves against the railing to let him pass. He saw the captain walk by and lifted his hand to catch his attention.

The captain glanced at him, but just as quickly glanced away. His expression said that he regretted making eye contact with the general.

What in the name of all that's holy? Gálvez thought.

The captain, seeing him approach, disappeared into the pilothouse.

Gálvez paused and thought back to the sailor with the sling and the four prisoners. Had something happened onboard? Was Lorenzo hurt? Gálvez stepped into the pilothouse.

"Captain," he said.

The captain had his back to him and jumped to hear Gálvez's voice. He swiveled. All color drained from his face. "Your Excellency."

The man was so rattled, he forgot to render a salute.

"Where is Major Bannister?" Gálvez kept his voice low and non-threatening.

"Your Excellency . . . eh . . . You see . . . eh . . . "

"Out with it, man!"

"I regret to say that we . . . eh . . . lost Major Bannister."

Gálvez's heart stopped. He thought he would be sick. Lorenzo . . . dead. That was impossible. The boy he had brought into his house three years earlier, his ward. Dead. Oh, God, Gálvez groaned inwardly. I sent him on this mission. I sent him to his death.

"How did he die?" Gálvez rasped.

"He's not dead. At least not as far as I know. I said we lost him."

It took a moment to grasp that. Gálvez frowned. "You lost him? Do you mean you misplaced him?"

The captain scratched the nape of his neck. "Not exactly. He boarded a pirate ship to care for a sick man. I told him not to go, but Major Bannister insisted."

That sounded like Lorenzo. More than one rash decision had landed him in desperate straits.

The captain continued. "A storm came up while the major was on the other ship. When it was over, the Liberty was nowhere in sight."

Gálvez's eyebrows shot up. "The Liberty?"

"A three-masted schooner with three cannon."

Gálvez knew the Liberty and had received word that it was on its way to New Orleans. It carried a chest that he needed desperately.

"And where is Major Bannister now?" Gálvez asked.

The captain's gaze went to a faraway spot. "I don't exactly

know, but I can give you an estimate." The captain unfurled a map on the chart table.

Gálvez bent over it.

"Given the prevailing winds," the captain said, "their strength, direction, sea currents, our location when the storm began—"

"Yes, yes, get on with it."

"He's probably near the Yucatan Peninsula."

"Probably," Gálvez said. "Can you narrow that down?"

The young sailor with a monkey saved him the trouble of a response. He thrust his head into the pilothouse and said, "Begging the captain's pardon, but I don't know what to do with the m—" He froze. His eyes swept Gálvez, from his three-cornered hat to his shiny black boots.

Gálvez had experienced this reaction to his rank before and he found it irritating. People assumed that he was frigid and distant because of his social standing and military rank. The people of New Orleans had learned better in the last three years. Strangers still treated him with overblown courtesy and fear.

"Come in, Francisco," the captain said, obviously welcoming the interruption.

Wide-eyed, the boy shuffled toward them like a man on the way to his execution.

"This is Francisco, my cabin boy," the captain said. "He is from Andalucía, born and raised not far from Your Excellency's hometown."

"Where are you from?" Gálvez asked the boy.

"S . . . S . . . Sevilla," the boy stammered out.

"Ah, yes, beautiful town. What is the monkey's name?"

"I don't know. I mean, it's not mine, but I wish he were. He's kind of cute." He offered an orange slice that the beast grabbed and ate. "It belongs to Major Bannister."

Gálvez tilted his head. "Major Bannister?"

"Yes, Your Excellency. A Christmas present for his wife. I've been taking care of it since the major left."

"Take it to my house, son," Gálvez said. "Give it to Mrs. Bannister. Tell my wife to give you something to eat."

"Yes, Your Excellency."

"After you drop off the monkey, come back to the ship, pick up your sea bag, and report to my office. I have a special mission for you."

"Eh . . . eh," the captain said, lifting an index finger in the air.

Gálvez swiveled toward him. "Do you have something to say?"

"Francisco is my personal cabin boy."

"Losing your cabin boy is the price you pay for losing my major."

The captain seemed to realize that protest was useless. Gálvez outranked him.

He would have to send a second envoy to Havana to learn the Captain General's response to the request for supplies and ships. The perfect person sprang to mind: Lieutenant Colonel Estéban Miró. It usually took three or four days to unload and load cargo. The ship had to take on provisions for the trip back to Cuba. Miró would be onboard.

And then there was the problem of Captain Slaughter's chest. Pondering this, Gálvez walked out of the pilothouse. He needed to find Lorenzo. Finding the chest was equally important. He spotted Thomas on deck picking up a mailbag. "Thomas," he called.

He trotted over. "Yes, Your Excellency?"

"Are you heading to Baton Rouge soon?"

"As soon as I get the mail sorted."

"Stop at Major Calderón's house and tell him to report to me at once."

"Certainly, Your Excellency."

Héctor Calderón and Lorenzo were like brothers. He would move heaven and earth to find Lorenzo.

Chapter Sixteen

1 have mixed emotions about the portrait," Héctor said to Davy Morgan as he slipped a key in the front door of the Hawthorne House. "In a way, I hate to give it up. It seems to belong to the house. On the other hand, I can understand why Colonel Hawthorne wants it."

"It is very gracious of you to let him have it."

Héctor waved the remark away and gestured for Morgan to go ahead of him.

The young man entered and looked around in awe. "Nice house."

Héctor accepted the compliment with a small nod. Sometimes he felt like a guest and not the owner. Everyone in town referred to it as the Hawthorne House, and Héctor could not bring himself to correct them. Perhaps removing the portrait would make it feel like it was truly his.

The house and grounds had been a spoil of war. The Hawthorne plantation consisted of ten arpents, about eight

English acres, and had a sawmill, fifty cabins for slaves, a stable for twelve horses, a large pigsty, an outhouse, barn, and smokehouse. One day while walking the property, Héctor had stumbled upon a slave cemetery with nineteen graves marked with simple white crosses. Someone had carved the name of each slave along with the date of death. All of them perished in the first week of April 1779.

"The portrait is in here," Héctor said, heading to the parlor. He paused by the crate in a rocking chair. "These are some things I found around the house. The colonel might want them." He pulled out two dolls, one with a porcelain face and a starched dress, the other a rag doll that had been loved to death. "And I assume this belonged to Evan." He indicated a leather medical bag. "I also found a ledger where the master of the house kept expenses." Héctor opened it and showed it to Morgan. "He was a very methodical man."

"I see." Morgan's gaze fixed on the portrait hanging above the parlor fireplace. It showed Evan Hawthorne in the background, his hand on his wife's shoulder. Seated on her lap was their child, Abigail. Morgan took several tentative steps toward it. "So that is the colonel's brother. He looks quite the decent chap."

Similar thoughts had run through Héctor's mind. If the artist had captured the true spirit of the man, then Evan Hawthorne had lacked the hardness and win-at-all-cost nature of his brother, Robert, or his cousin, Saber-Scar.

"Help me take it down," Héctor said to Morgan, going to the portrait.

Together they unhooked it from the wall. Ropes of dust and dirt roiled up.

Morgan took out a handkerchief and ran it over the frame. "Been a while since it's seen a cleaning."

"I haven't touched it since I moved . . ." The rest of the sentence evaporated. Héctor stood staring at a wall safe suddenly revealed by the picture's removal.

"What have we here?" Morgan asked.

Héctor turned the handle, expecting to find it locked, but it was not. The tiny door swung open. He glanced around at Morgan, who nodded encouragement. He reached inside and withdrew a small book. Héctor blew on the cover and dust plumed into the air. For a long moment, he held it as if it were a sacred religious icon. He opened to the first page. It was dated April 1, 1779.

"Major Calderón?" Morgan asked. "Are you all right?"

"This is Evan Hawthorne's diary."

Morgan moved to Héctor's side so he could read along with him.

April 1st.

The move from Natchez is complete. The last of our baggage has finally arrived from upriver. Toby is sick. I fear he has the pox. I have isolated him in a cabin at the back of the plantation away from the other slaves. Josephine insists upon taking the elderly fellow broth and bread. We argued. I could not persuade her otherwise. She says it is her duty as mistress of the plantation to care for the sick. If she catches the pox, whatever shall I do?

Héctor turned the page.

> *April 2nd.*
> *Three more slaves have taken to their beds. I nailed a sign to the front gate warning would-be visitors that there is a contagion on the grounds.*

> *April 3rd.*
> *Toby died today. We buried him in the cemetery at the back of the plantation. He leaves behind a wife and three children. Four more slaves have the pox. I have prohibited Abigail from playing with the slave children. Poor thing has no playmates. Josephine and I have barely had a chance to meet our new neighbors, and now this. Luckily, we have enough food in stock to last until the illness passes.*

> *April 4th.*
> *Josephine is ill. I had to leave her side to dig graves for three slaves. Cesar, Moses, and Hannibal are lost to us and now reside in the bosom of the Lord. Abigail and I are the only ones not infected. I pray, oh God how I pray, that she will not catch this.*

April 5th.

Abigail was playing outside when she cried out for her mother. I dashed outside and found her collapsed by the well, her face flushed. She has the pox. Oh, God, when will this plague end?

April 6th.

The last slave has died. Nineteen in all, gone to meet their Maker. Why can I not save them? Why must they die?

April 7th.

I left Josephine and Abigail's bedside for a moment and returned to find Josephine gone. My sweet, sweet Josephine. I thought we would grow old together surrounded by children and grandchildren. If we had not left Natchez, if we had not come to this God-forsaken town, she would be alive. Abigail is slipping away. I pray for a miracle.

The grim tale ended at that point. The rest of the pages were empty.

"*Válgame,*" Héctor heard himself say. His chest constricted. He tried to erase the image of a man burying twenty-one people in five days, but could not.

There were only two graves in the family cemetery. What had become of Evan? Had he come down with the pox too? Was his body lying somewhere around the plantation waiting to be discovered? Héctor thought he had examined the property thoroughly. Had he missed something?

"May I have that, sir?" Morgan asked, pulling the diary from him.

"*Sí, sí, por supuesto.*" Héctor released it, only then realizing that he held it in an iron grip. "Let's get the portrait packed on your wagon so you can be on your way."

They carried the painting out to the wagon and covered it with a tarpaulin to protect it from the weather.

Héctor shook hands with Morgan and wished him a speedy journey.

Morgan hopped to the driver's seat and drove off.

For several minutes, Héctor stood staring at the Hawthorne House. It had lost much of its charm, now that he knew it was a plague house.

Chapter Seventeen

R eaching Cozumel seemed to take forever. Lorenzo passed no landmarks to give him a sense of progress. At some point, his brain stopped working and each stroke became exactly like the one before. There was only one goal: dry land.

Fins passed on his left and right. At first, his heart sank, thinking that the shark had returned and had brought re-enforcements. Then, Lorenzo's dark gray companions jumped out of the water and twittered. It took several seconds to get over his initial fear and realize he was in the middle of a dolphin herd. Herd? Flock? Pack? How did dolphins travel? Inwardly, he laughed at himself. Here he was, struggling for shore, trying hard not to drown, and he was worried about getting a word right.

Dolphins, a hundred or more, flowed past like a river, many of them close enough to reach out and touch. As quickly as they appeared, they disappeared.

He swam on and on. Looking down into the crystal-clear water, he saw starfish on the bottom of the sea. It looked like a starry sky in daylight. A little later, he touched sand. He splashed out of the water and struggled up the beach, his shirt and breeches clinging to his skin. He collapsed face up. Every muscle ached. His lungs burned from exhaustion. The scalpel wound on his left hand stung from the exposure to salt water.

But he was alive. He had made it!

After a short rest, he forced himself up. He looked for the three British warships, but they had sailed away.

He was all alone on a deserted island. No one knew where he was. He could be on this island for a day, a month, a year, or forever. The thought hit him like a hammer blow to the head. How far was Cozumel from the Mexican coast? Twelve miles? More? In his mind's eye, he saw the map Blackie had shown him. He doubted that he could swim to Mexico, but if he built a raft . . . He let the thought float away. ¡Tonto! If he was going to survive, he had to focus on immediate problems. He had never been shipwrecked on a tropical island, but he had been raised among soldiers and had learned how to survive in the harshest of conditions.

Water was his top priority. Next came shelter, then food. He recalled the bright yellow fish he had seen. The sea was alive with food. He scanned the thick undergrowth on the island. What kinds of animals lived there? He would need a fire at night for warmth and to keep unwelcomed guests away. The long knife Blackie had given him was his only tool and only defense against whatever lived on the island. He wished he had a hatchet. He opened the burlap sack and took out his boots. They were soggy and needed to dry out. The only object remaining was the swollen pig bladder that had kept the bag afloat.

Shadows from palm trees wandered across the sand and suggested it was early afternoon. The sun would go down in about six hours. That did not leave much time to build a shelter, at least not a permanent one. For now, a lean-to was ideal. He would work on a better shelter tomorrow.

Was he in an area where ships were likely to sail? How did he signal them?

Blackie said there were reefs on the west side of the island. That meant ships would prefer the east coast. At the moment, he was on the northernmost point of the island. If he had any chance of being rescued, he needed to stay near the shore so he could signal a passing ship.

Rested, he walked down the powder-soft beach on the east side of the coast and looked for a good place to spend the night.

The sun beat down on him. He wiped away sweat with his sleeve. I need a hat, he thought. His throat burned from all the salt water he had taken in. I need water more than I need a hat, he decided.

He happened upon a boulder about fifty yards from the sea. Palm trees swayed behind it. This would be an ideal place to camp.

He studied the closest palm tree a moment and remembered

Cuban boys scaling them like monkeys. The best coconuts were at the top of the tree. The ones on the ground had little water in them and the meat was hard. No use wasting energy on those.

Rubbing his hands together, he started to climb the tree. A few feet off the ground, he fell. He picked himself up and eyed the tree as if it were the enemy. He would not let a coconut tree defeat him.

How had Cuban boys done it? They scampered up tree trunks with no problem at all.

Frogs! That was it! They had hopped like frogs.

He put the soles of his feet flat against the trunk and his hands on the tree, one behind and the other in front at chest level, and pushed up with his feet. He moved his hands up the trunk and repeated the process. His feet supported most of his weight. He rested a few seconds and did it all again. He slowly inched up the tree. The strange technique became second nature by the time he reached the top and grabbed a coconut.

It was firmly attached to the tree. What now? Holding the tree tight with one hand, he twisted the coconut with the other until the stem broke and the nut fell. It plopped onto the sand. He broke off three more. They dropped and rolled in all directions.

He hopped down the tree. In spite of himself, he started laughing. This was hardly a gentlemanly way to get food and water, but at least no one had seen him lose his dignity.

He took out his long knife and whacked a V at the top of a coconut. The sweet juice felt good rolling down his throat. He loved the sugary taste. Next, he whacked the nut in half and scooped out the soft meat with a shell. He shoved it into his mouth. Delicious! Well worth the effort! He stacked coconuts like cannonballs next to the boulder.

That done, he set about planning a shelter. It would be hard work cutting wood with just his knife.

Lorenzo scoured the beach for driftwood, but there wasn't much. He would have to face the jungle. He put on his boots. Amazingly, they were sun-dried, only slightly damp on the inside. He ventured into the interior for lean, stout sticks. Trip after trip, he brought building material to the boulder. He took special care around fallen logs, aware that snakes and other critters liked to hide under them.

On his fifth trip, he felt a tiny prick in the sole of his foot. He sat down on the boulder and examined his boot. To his amazement, the sole was covered with thorns. They had penetrated the leather and just barely touched skin. He pulled them out, one by one. They looked like tiny nails. Lorenzo was glad Blackie had made sure he had boots. He could not have gone into the interior without them.

He stacked wood on the boulder and was about to go for more when a piece of driftwood about thirty feet from the shore caught his eye. It looked like something was hooked around one of its branches.

Lorenzo started to laugh. It couldn't be . . . He ran down the beach, dove into the water, and swam with all his might to the driftwood. He unhooked his amputation kit and wondered how it had become snagged on a tree.

Back on the beach, he opened the case. Water had seeped inside and had ruined the velvet interior, but the blades were unharmed. He dried them with his shirt and left the case open in the sun. Looking at the kit was bittersweet. He wished he had his father's medical bag as well. It had been with him for years, and he could not believe he had lost it.

For the first time, he realized that some of the flotsam from the Liberty might land on his beach. He decided to keep an eye out for useful things.

Using the saw, he cut off some low-lying tree branches and dragged them to the boulder. He leaned them against it and crawled underneath them to make sure there was enough room to sleep. Next, he piled debris over the slanted branches to insulate the lean-to.

He stood back and admired his work. It would make a suitable shelter for the night.

Using his hands to dig a fire pit in the sand made him feel like a dog digging a hole to bury a bone. First a frog, now a dog, he mused. A friend once told him: *If you keep your sense of humor, you can make it through most anything.*

Lorenzo ringed the top of the hole with seashells and filled it with twigs and sticks.

Satisfied that he had gathered enough material to last the night, he tried to start a fire by hitting two rocks together. He knew how to start a blaze with a tinderbox, but this was much harder. It took several attempts before he made a tiny spark catch on the tinder. He blew on it to encourage it to grow. Soon, flames licked the wood. He sat on the beach and watched the fire as it crackled and sputtered. The noise was comforting and blocked out the sounds of birds fussing and creatures moving in the jungle at his back.

Night fell. Stars filled the sky and blinked overhead.

By firelight, he made a torch and fashioned a spear from a long stick. He went down the beach, waded waist-high into the water, and held his torch over it.

Fish swam toward the light. He held his spear at the ready and waited. He stabbed and missed. He stabbed again. And again. And again. And again. Frustrated, he let out a small growl. There were fish everywhere! And then, it occurred to him. The burlap bag. Of course! What a dolt he was! He waded ashore, dashed to the lean-to, and grabbed the burlap bag. At the water's edge, he thrust the torch into the sand and left it burning. By its flickering light, he waded into the water, held the bag open, and in no time watched a fat fish about a foot long swim into it. "Yes!" Lorenzo exclaimed as he snapped the bag shut. He carried the flopping fish back to the lean-to where he speared it and placed it over the fire to roast.

While waiting for it to cook, he listened to the waves washing over the beach and the squawk of sea gulls anxious to steal his food. This was a fine spot he had gotten himself into. He did not regret going on the Liberty to give the captain medical care. It was the right thing to do. His only regret was the worry he was causing Eugenie. The San Juan Nepomuceno must have reached New Orleans by now.

And then there was the general to consider. No doubt, he was pacing about, alternately praying for Lorenzo's safe return and cursing him for making a side trip to the pirate ship. I can say farewell to future promotions, Lorenzo told himself as he pulled the cooked fish from the fire and blew on it. My mission to Cuba was a failure. I did not get a promise for troops and supplies, but I was right about the reason the Captain General was dragging his feet.

He thought back to the night he and the general had played billiards in the Saint Maxent house. It was after midnight. Everyone else had retired for the night, but the general, as usual, was a bundle of energy. He wanted to talk about war plans and had invited Lorenzo for a game of billiards.

Gálvez had graciously allowed Lorenzo to take the first shot. They had played several rounds in silence.

"I hear Héctor is courting," Gálvez said, as he bent over the table and prepared his next shot.

Lorenzo stopped chalking his cue stick. Didn't anything escape the general's attention?

Gálvez glanced up. "Do you know the girl?"

"Yes, sir. Eugenie and I introduced him to her."

Billiard balls clacked together as Gálvez took his shot. "Does she have any brothers of fighting age?"

Lorenzo struggled not to smile. "Beating the bushes, are we, sir?"

"If it breathes, is old enough to carry a musket, and isn't

British, it's a candidate for recruitment. As soon as everything is in place, I am going after Mobile."

"Not Pensacola?"

"I would like to go for the lion's throat and end this once and for all, but I don't have enough troops."

Lorenzo felt a smile growing and tried to hide it.

Gálvez scowled at him. "I know. I know. I have danced to that tune before. The Captain General is still dragging his feet."

"Why?"

A long breath of disgust had been Gálvez's only answer.

Now, in light of all Lorenzo had learned on his trip to Cuba, he suspected there was a personality conflict between Don Bernardo and Navarro, the Captain General. Navarro appeared to be jealous of Gálvez's success. He told Lorenzo he could not help Don Bernardo because Havana had supported the military operations of his father, Matías de Gálvez, in Honduras.

Lorenzo understood the unspoken jab. Don Bernardo's father had lost the Battle of Omoa to the British in October of 1779.

Navarro came up with a litany of excuses for not giving Don Bernardo aid. First, the fleet could not sail because of the weather. Then, the soldiers needed capes. And finally, he criticized Gálvez for naming a good friend, Colonel José de Ezpeleta, as the commanding officer of the battalion.

For Lorenzo, that was the last straw. It made perfect sense for Gálvez to want a trusted friend at his side when he attacked Mobile!

Navarro wasn't the only one dragging his feet. Talking to Juan Bautista Bonet, commander of naval forces in Cuba, proved just as fruitless.

"Havana is worth fifty Mobiles," Bonet had told Lorenzo. "We cannot leave it defenseless. You must understand that I have responsibilities other than New Orleans. General Gálvez will have to do the best he can under the circumstances."

Bonet was openly defying the king and acting contrary to his Royal Orders to strike the British. Lorenzo found that astounding. The king wanted an expedition of sea and land forces to attack Mobile and Pensacola without delay.

So did General Washington. In September 1779, he had received reports from privateers who had recently returned from the Caribbean. Lorenzo idly wondered if one of them had been Captain Slaughter and the crew of the Liberty.

Washington understood the importance of capturing Pensacola and urged the Spanish to attack the forts at Mobile and Pensacola. That would force the British to shift their war effort away from the colonies and would take the pressure off American forces.

The plan was working. The war was moving south. British units had already begun embarking from New York and sailing for East Florida and the West Indies.

Navarro and Bonet thoroughly disgusted Lorenzo. The Spanish government—which included Don Bernardo's highly influential uncle—wanted them to act decisively against the British. Still, Havana hesitated and debated.

Don Bernardo was not the kind of man to sit on his hands and wait for others to make up their minds.

Lorenzo took one final look at the sky ablaze with stars. Don Bernardo was the kind of man who would send a rescue mission as soon as he learned that Lorenzo was missing. Even so, rescue was a long shot.

Tired, sore from work, he stretched out full length in the lean-to, rested his head on his hands, and fell asleep dreaming of Eugenie.

Chapter Eighteen

At dawn, Héctor Calderón boarded the Santa Ana and inspected it from bow to stern. General Gálvez had given him the ten-gun ship so he could look for Lorenzo. Technically, it was not a ship, for it only had two masts, and it was far from seaworthy. Héctor went down into the hold and looked around. It would take weeks of hard work to get her ready to sail. The general wanted the fleet to sail by January 10th. Today was December 17th. Héctor hoped his ship would be seaworthy by then, but doubted it. He was to take the Santa Ana to the mouth of the Mississippi, then sail toward the Yucatan in hopes of locating Lorenzo and the chest.

By the time Héctor returned to the quarterdeck, he found the general leaning against a railing, looking at New Orleans the way a man admired a pretty woman.

"What do you think of your ship?" Gálvez asked.

Héctor tried to hide his disappointment, but the general was an expert at reading faces.

"Out with it," the general said.

"It's a barge, Your Excellency. I have more rats than crewmen."

Gálvez laughed. "Do you really think so?"

"I think I should rename it the Eversink. I also think you are sending me on a fool's quest."

The general's usual jolly disposition dissolved. "I pray not. Lorenzo is alive. I feel it in my bones."

After three years of service under Gálvez, Héctor knew that the general's gut feelings were always on target.

Lorenzo had survived a cattle stampede, a hurricane, and capture by the British. Héctor had to admit that it was hard to imagine him being killed by a little thing like a storm at sea. Lorenzo also had an uncanny knack for getting into trouble. Three years earlier, Héctor had the dubious honor of arresting him for brawling on the streets of New Orleans with three British soldiers.

"The ship needs repairs," Héctor said.

"Unfortunately, yes," Gálvez said, "but it is the only vessel I can spare. Perhaps Lorenzo will show up and you will be spared a fool's quest."

Héctor hoped he was right.

"The American sailors should be along shortly," Gálvez added. "Last night when I released them, they gave their word of honor to report at seven o'clock sharp. One of them has a brother on the Liberty and volunteered on the spot. The other three agreed to go as well, partly out of loyalty to their shipmates, partly because they wanted to ship out as soon as they could."

"They don't like New Orleans?" Héctor asked.

"It loses some of its charm when you see it from a jail cell."

Three young men with sea bags over their shoulders headed toward the Santa Ana.

"Ah, here come your sailors now," Gálvez said.

Héctor stared, disbelieving his eyes. "They are children!"

"Indeed not! They are American fighting men."

Mary, Joseph, and Jesus, Calderón thought. The general is turning me into a nursemaid. None of the three young sailors was over twenty.

A sideways look at the general showed him scowling at the sailors.

"This is not good news," he said to Héctor. "One of your sailors is missing. A man named Josiah Crowe."

Chapter Nineteen

L orenzo opened his eyes, groaned, and crawled out of the lean-to. Facing the rising sun, he stretched to erase the stiffness from sleeping on the ground. During the night, the fire had gone out. He restarted it and searched for food. With a sea full of fish, crabs, lobster, and shellfish and an island laden with cashew nuts, berries, pineapples, and other delicious plants, he would not starve to death. He found two bird eggs and placed them in the embers. While they cooked, he started to weave a hat out of palm leaves.

He tried to concentrate on the task, but his mind took him back to the British shooting Blackie's sailors. It was a tragic loss of life. For the first time, he felt pangs of remorse for being alive. Why had he survived while they had perished? So he could die of loneliness on a deserted island?

He bent over the hat, his fingers working feverishly. Stop feeling sorry for yourself! You've been in tighter spots than this. "I refuse to give up," he said in a loud, firm voice. "I refuse to feel guilty about something I cannot control."

Saying the words made him feel better.

He put on his new hat and checked the eggs roasting in ashes.

The rest of the day, to ward off depressing thoughts, he sang while he worked. It was amazing how many songs he knew, some of them English tunes his father had taught him, some of them Spanish folk songs he had learned as a boy, and still others were French ones Eugenie often sang.

By noon, he had fashioned a bow and had strung it with thick thread from the amputation kit. He set about making arrows.

That done, he looked at his lean-to and decided it was time to build a better shelter. Whistling a happy tune, he headed to the closest vegetation and yanked down some vines. He carried them to camp, where he tore off the leaves. He found a Y-shaped tree branch perfect to use as a vertical brace and dragged it to the beach.

He dug a hole in the ground and thrust the branch into it with the Y sticking straight up. It fell over before he could pat sand around it. He dug the hole a little deeper and held the pole with one hand while shoveling sand around it with the other. It fell again. He tried again, this time bracing the base with coco-nuts. It fell.

"I give up!" he yelled. Frustrated, tired, and lonely, he flopped down on the ground.

The sun was dropping toward the horizon. At this rate, night would fall before the shelter was finished. He was a major in the army, raised around Apaches and soldiers, trained to survive in the worst of situations, and he couldn't do a simple task like building a stupid hut!

He picked up seashells and angrily hurled them into the sea. I want to be back in civilization! I want to go home! I want to be with Eugenie! I'm never going to see her again. I'm going to die on this God-forsaken island. My bones will bleach, and no one will know what became of me.

He thought about the piece of property he and Eugenie had chosen beyond the French Gate at the down-river corner of the city. We will never build the house we talked about. It is prime real estate. Someone will buy it before we do.

He and Eugenie had spent hours designing a home made of cypress planks and beams set high off the ground. It would have two stories with upper galleries on all four sides, seven columns per side, two dormers, two chimneys, a lightning rod, and a curving staircase.

"Our house must have many bedrooms," Eugenie had said.

"Why?"

"For our children."

He had eyed her suspiciously. "How many are you planning on?"

She shrugged. "Seven . . . eight."

"Seven?"

"Or eight. Not all at the same time, *mon petit choux*."

He blew out an exaggerated breath. "That's a relief."

He could understand her longing for a big family. He had been an only child and often wished he had brothers and sisters. Like Eugenie, he had found himself unexpectedly alone, left to fend for himself.

Just like now.

Lorenzo stood and walked down the beach, hands laced behind his back. From time to time, he flung a shell into the sea. Seeing an odd-shaped one, he picked it up, but before he hurled it in frustration, he noticed it held a little sea creature. Only the claws were visible.

Lorenzo studied the terrified creature for a moment, laughed, shook his head, and carefully put it back. If God had given a little crab shelter for the night, he would surely give Lorenzo protection too.

He looked at the pile of building material waiting for him. The hut would not assemble itself.

He went back to his soon-to-be-built hut and picked up a vine. It made a tune pop into mind. "To Anacreon in Heaven," a song he learned in Philadelphia, ended with something about entwining vines. If all went well, Lorenzo would entwine this vine around the Y-shaped branch and the cross beam. Lorenzo struggled to remember the words as he lashed wood together. He sang, putting in "dum-de-dums" when he couldn't remember the words.

To Anacreon in Heav'n
Where he sat in full glee,

(dum-de-dum dee dee dum
dum de dum dum dum dum dum)
Voice, Fiddle and Flute,
No longer be mute
I'll lend you my name
And inspire you to boot.
And besides I'll instruct you,
Like me, to entwine,
The myrtle of (de dum)
And (dum de dum's) vine.

The song did not make a lot of sense, but it was, after all, a drinking song, and who expected them to be truly inspired works of art?

Lorenzo sang it again, hoping to recall the missing words. Instead, faintly in the distance, he heard someone singing the same tune. Whoever it was knew all the words. Lorenzo tilted his head to determine the direction of the singing. He shaded his eyes and saw two figures on the beach coming from the north.

One hobbled along leaning on the other who had an arm around his waist. The second man was bare-chested, wore an oilskin pouch around his neck, and held something in his free hand, something that looked very familiar.

Overjoyed, Lorenzo broke into a run. His bare feet pounded the sand.

"Lorenzo!" one of the men yelled.

"*¡Dichosos los ojos que los ven!*" Realizing he had slipped into Spanish, Lorenzo said, "Am I glad to see you two!" He had known Blackie and Abercrombie for a mere two days but he had never been so glad to see anyone in his life. He pulled them into a hug.

"We heard caterwauling," Blackie said, grinning, "and thought someone was in pain. We beached on the west side. If you had not been singing, we would not have known you had made it to shore. Here." Blackie shoved the medical bag toward Lorenzo. "This washed ashore."

Lorenzo clutched the bag and pulled Blackie into another bone-crushing hug.

Abercrombie limped to the boulder and eased down. He grimaced in pain.

"What happened to him?" Lorenzo asked, nodding toward the boy's foot. It was bound in black linen. He assumed Blackie had used his shirt to make the bandage.

Blackie's jaw tightened. "The bastards shot him. They put sharpshooters in the ship's rigging! Britain is the most civilized country in the world. We brag about our sense of fair play. But what do we do? We slaughter unarmed men!"

Lorenzo said nothing. He had lost Red, his best friend, in a massacre. The British had trapped Red and other soldiers in a house in New Jersey. The attack was so vicious, blood dripped from the ceiling.

"The sharks ate them," Blackie mumbled.

His voice was so soft, Lorenzo had to strain to hear. He suddenly recalled the shark that had menaced him. It had veered away

136

from him and had swum off unexpectedly. The blood in the water must have drawn him away. Lorenzo wondered why Abercrombie had survived with a wounded foot oozing blood, but then recalled that survival sometimes depended on dumb luck.

"This will not stand," Blackie said, his voice suddenly angry. "I shall see my sailors avenged. They were no threat. The British should have taken them prisoner, but they shot them like mad dogs in the street!"

Lorenzo had never seen Blackie so agitated. Surprised by the angry tirade, he studied him a moment. It was as if a dam of emotions had burst inside him and had gushed out in words.

"Captain Slaughter was right," Blackie said in a slightly calmer voice. "He encouraged me to declare myself for the colonies. I straddled the fence, not knowing which side I should fall on. Should I be loyal to the man who helped me in my hour of need or should I remain loyal to Mother England? I found myself sailing hither and yon, delivering messages to rebels, burying a chest to keep it out of British hands, committing treason at the captain's behest." A muscle worked in Blackie's jaw. "As of this moment, I am a rebel."

Lorenzo did not know what to say to that. He wanted to say *Welcome aboard*, but it sounded flippant under the circumstances.

Side by side, Lorenzo and Blackie stood looking at the sea. The awkward moment stretched. Lorenzo searched for a way to break the silence.

"I'm hungry," Abercrombie called from his perch on the

boulder. "Do you have anything to eat, Doctor Bannister?"

"I have some fruit at the foot of that palm."

"What about those?" Abercrombie pointed to the pile of coconuts holding up one of the hut's posts.

"Touch those coconuts and I will skin you alive and tan your hide."

"I'm hungry!" the boy said, crossing his arms over his chest and sticking out his lower lip.

"Fruit," Lorenzo said. "Under the palm."

Giving Lorenzo a less-than-charitable look, he hobbled over to it.

"Come on, *compadre*," Lorenzo said, patting Blackie on the back. "Let's get something to eat."

Abercrombie munched on a piece of fruit. "Here, Mr. B.," he said, tossing one to Blackie who caught it.

"You are a gentleman and a scholar." He examined it a second before biting into it. "Looks like you're building a hut," he mumbled around a mouthful of fruit. "Need help?"

"I could use a hand," Lorenzo said. He knew their situation was desperate, but not hopeless. At least now he had companionship.

Chapter Twenty

Where was that damn chest?

Hands locked behind his back, Augustus Fitzgibbons rocked his heels over the frigate's quarterdeck and went over the information in his head looking for a clue. For the hundredth time in two months, he reviewed everything he knew so far. Twenty thousand dollars in gold had been onboard the Liberty. Twenty thousand! Augustus had never seen that much money in his entire life and could not fathom what it looked like.

Fathom. Augustus silently cursed his word choice. Did the gold now lie several fathoms below at the bottom of the sea?

He needed information and he needed it now. The trail began six months earlier in Charlottesville, Virginia, with a barmaid who overheard a conversation between Captain Slaughter and a man in his seventies. From what she gleaned of the conversation, there was something important the old man wanted transported to New Orleans.

Being a good Tory, she passed the information along to Augustus. He investigated and discovered that Captain Slaughter had made an extraordinary number of trips from Virginia to the Gulf of Mexico. After the King of Spain declared war on Great Britain in June of 1779, Augustus grew even more suspicious of the captain.

His gaze swept the frigate's main deck. He had wasted six months on this affair. Augustus wanted it over now.

Two marines stood guard at the metal grating. In the hold below were two pirates rescued from the sea.

He had sprung the trap nicely. The Liberty was too fast to be captured by speed. Only trickery had brought her down. He hadn't expected her to blow up. He idly wondered if Josiah Crowe, his man onboard, still lived. He had known Josiah, a fellow Bostonian, from the cradle.

Lieutenant Sparks, recently promoted from midshipman, had the watch. At seventeen, he was half Augustus's age. Augustus knew he was getting old when men Sparks's age looked like babies.

Augustus strode to the officer of the deck. "Fly the yellow flag."

"Sir?" Lieutenant Sparks swallowed so hard his Adam's apple bounced.

"The yellow flag."

"But sir—"

Augustus put his face very close to the officer's. Their three-cornered hats nearly collided. "I would have sworn I heard you say something. Did you say something, Sparks?"

The officer avoided looking at him. His eyes took on the glazed look of a man trying very hard to keep his composure.

"I thought not. Fly the flag and prepare the men."

The officer's eyes darted to and fro like an animal unexpectedly freed from a cage. He touched his hat in salute. "By your command, sir."

Augustus stepped aside and made a sweeping motion with his hand.

Sparks strode from the quarterdeck spitting out orders that made sailors and marines scramble to assigned posts.

Augustus had long ago concluded that the lieutenant was a good man made predictable by a sense of conscience. Son of a vicar, he was burdened with unenlightened concepts like honor, duty, and fair play. He had protested Augustus's order to shoot the Liberty's sailors and had received a dressing down from the captain for his efforts. Smart man, the captain. He knew which way the wind was blowing.

The head of British intelligence had given Augustus free rein to find the chest. That included the ability to commandeer three ships to hunt down the Liberty. From the captain to the cabin boy, every man knew that Augustus had the power of life or death over them. They were terrified of a man who could board a frigate, flash a piece of paper under the captain's nose, and take over the ship.

Not bad for a cobbler's son, Augustus thought.

Augustus waited with infinite patience as marines fell in,

making a double file on the starboard side from the quarterdeck to the forecastle. When all was in place, Augustus gave the order, "Bring one of them up."

"Which one, sir?"

"The blond."

The metal grating screeched. A guard disappeared down the stairs.

Augustus hated blonds. They reminded him of his wife who had hair the color of a new straw hat.

The marine reappeared a moment later with a prisoner, his hands shackled behind him. The young man stumbled, barefoot, onto the deck. He blinked repeatedly as his eyes adjusted to the light. The prisoner peered left and right. The flapping of the yellow flag, the flag of capital punishment, drew the prisoner's gaze upwards.

The man paled. Terror filled his eyes.

Augustus leaned toward him, as if about to share a confidence. "You can avoid this nasty affair. Tell me where the chest is."

"I don't know nothing 'bout no chest."

"Someone is going to die today," Augustus whispered. "Tell me where it is and your companion takes your place."

Sweat beaded on the sailor's forehead and rolled into his eyes. "Mr. Blackie buried it on Isla Mujeres."

"Where exactly?"

The man lifted a shoulder.

Augustus struggled to control his rage. Isla Mujeres was

about five miles long. He needed an exact location. Otherwise, he would have to dig up the entire island to find it. Augustus let out an extravagant sigh. "And they say ignorance is bliss. In your case, ignorance is deadly." He spoke to the marine. "Take him to the place of execution."

The prisoner swayed. "No! Please! I can find it. Take me to Isla Mujeres. I watched them row Mr. B. to the island. I know where they landed."

"Mr. B.?"

"Mister B., the quartermaster."

Damn, damn, damn, damn, damn. Did this Mr. B. now reside in the bowels of some shark? Augustus silently cursed. At the time, killing the pirates seemed a good idea.

He had been so angry, seeing the pirates blow up the ship and the $20,000! The order to shoot to kill was out before he knew what he was saying.

Acting first, thinking of the consequences later . . . That had been a problem even when he was a clerk in Boston. He had been dismissed from one position after another until he found the perfect one: working for the intelligence service.

After he engineered the massacre at the Hancock House, respect for his talents swelled among the British. Still, they treated him like half-a-man because he was a colonial. He could bear their insults. Anything was better than clerking.

With a flick of the hand, Augustus indicated that the marines were to take the condemned man to the place of execution. The marines gripped the pirate by the upper arms and propelled him to the noose dangling from the yardarm. Wedged between two marines, the prisoner passed through men lining his path. He appeared to be in denial, not completely understanding what was about to happen.

The execution was a last minute plan. There was no warrant of execution. No one read the sentence of the court. The prisoner was not given a final interview with the chaplain. The crew was not required to attend the execution, for it was not for their benefit. It was meant for the prisoner in the hold.

The boatswain's mate placed a noose around the pirate's neck and adjusted it. At last, the condemned man seemed to understand his fate. He struggled to get away, but the marines held him fast.

Augustus took a white handkerchief from his pocket. At his signal, the boatswain's mate nodded to two sailors. They pulled on the rope, jerking the man up and lifting him midway between the deck and the yardarm. There was a strangled cry. His body quivered, then went limp.

Augustus watched the man swing from the yardarm. The chap had gone to his death revealing nothing. Bother! "Lower him," Augustus said to the boatswain's mate. "Throw him into the hold."

For a full five seconds, no one moved. Scarce a word was heard. The boatswain's mate glanced at Lieutenant Sparks, still standing on the quarterdeck. Sparks gave a barely perceptible nod.

His scowl warmed Augustus's heart. No doubt, he

wanted to give the corpse a Christian burial. Augustus congratulated himself. He knew he was doing well when Sparks disapproved.

Sailors removed the rope, carried the dead man to the metal grating, and dumped the body into the dark.

A cry of horror burst from the hold.

The grating was put back in place.

It was Augustus's sincerest hope that the surviving pirate would tell what he knew and save him the trouble of another execution. It would take a day or two to reach Mobile. Perhaps by that time, the man in the hold would loosen his tongue.

Chapter Twenty-One

Dusk settled over Cozumel. Lorenzo and Blackie sat on the beach and watched a sea gull roast over the fire. Abercrombie lay nearby looking up at the stars.

"A backgammon match before supper?" Blackie asked.

"Why not?"

They had been on the island for a week and playing backgammon had become a nightly ritual.

Blackie drew a design in the sand. "Do you remember how to set up the board?"

"Of course I do." Lorenzo was not sure at all, but he was not going to admit it. He placed the shells and nuts that they used as playing pieces in the sand and looked up.

Blackie shook his head and moved pieces to their correct positions. "Spaniards. Too proud for their own good."

"I'm Mexican," Lorenzo pointed out.

"If you're from New Spain, that makes you a New Spaniard."

"I'm Mexican," Lorenzo insisted, "and I cannot wait until we get our independence from Spain . . . just like the Americans."

"Roll the dice." Blackie handed him a pair carved out of bones.

Lorenzo threw double sixes. He knew it was an excellent roll and suppressed a victorious smile.

Blackie snorted. "You have the luck of the Irish."

"I'm Mexican, remember?"

Blackie blew on the dice and threw them. He took his turn.

"Must you blow on the dice?" Lorenzo gingerly picked them up.

"It improves my luck."

Lorenzo gave the dice a good shaking and threw them. "I think we should build a raft."

Blackie looked up sharply. "Would you kindly drop the idea? You mention it every night."

"If we sail to the mainland, we can walk up the coastline to the nearest port and hop a ship."

"In my humble yet accurate opinion, that is folly. It is better to wait here for a ship to pass and hail it. Need I mention that we lack the necessary tools to construct a raft?"

"Are you going to let a little thing like that stand in your way?"

Blackie lifted his hands to the sky as if asking for divine intervention. "Roll the dice, please."

Not having a hatchet was a major obstacle to Lorenzo's raft-building proposal. His amputation saw was not the right size to cut down the big trees they needed. Building a raft was a moot point anyway. Basic survival tasks absorbed most of each day—gathering firewood and kindling, making weapons, fishing, hunting, and hauling fresh water from a pond in the interior. By dusk, they were always too tired to tackle the project.

From time to time, they retrieved items that floated ashore. Some were useful, like a barrel filled with soggy flour. They rinsed out the barrel and used it for water. Other items had been useful in a different way. A crate of water-soaked bonnets, handbags, and paper fans became the source of numerous jokes.

Saddest of all, a drowned sailor washed onto the beach. He had not been shot. That fact gave Blackie hope that some of his men had gotten away.

At night, Lorenzo gave Blackie and Abercrombie Spanish lessons while they sat around the campfire weaving baskets and making arrows. He called it sink-or-swim Spanish. He talked, gestured, and acted out words and phrases. Some concepts were easy. When he said "fuego" and pointed to the campfire, their faces brightened with understanding. But when he said, "guapo" and patted his face, they seemed not to grasp the concept. Eugenie said he was handsome. Apparently, it was not an opinion held by all.

Abercrombie turned out to be a dull-witted fellow who did not have a thirst for knowledge. Blackie, on the other hand, proved an apt pupil who picked up Spanish as if it were second nature.

"How did you learn to play backgammon?" Lorenzo asked as he captured one of Blackie's seashells and sent it to the bar.

"I don't recall."

It was his normal response to any question about his past. At first, Lorenzo watched what he said, not wishing to put Blackie on the spot, but after a while, he abandoned all pretense at politeness. He could not tiptoe around every subject. Quite possibly he would stumble upon the thing that would jog Blackie's memory.

"It's almost Christmas," Lorenzo said.

"Truly?" Blackie scowled at the backgammon board where Lorenzo had two of his pieces trapped.

"Hey, Abercrombie. What is today's date?"

"December 24th, sir. Christmas Eve."

Lorenzo gave Blackie a smug look.

Abercrombie's wound prevented him from physical labor, so he became the camp cook and official timekeeper. Every day, he made a notch on a stick to mark the passing of time.

"How do you celebrate Christmas in England?" Lorenzo asked.

"We kill the Christmas goose and roast it. In the present circumstances, I suppose we will have to kill the Christmas pelican."

Lorenzo rubbed his hand over his face and wished he had a razor. The longer they stayed on the island, the longer their beards became. Abercrombie wasn't old enough to have anything but fuzz on his face, but Lorenzo and Blackie needed a shave. Lorenzo tried to dry shave one day with an amputation knife, but knicked himself and resigned himself to the discomfort of a beard.

Clothing was rapidly becoming a problem. They had arrived on the island wearing only shirts, knee britches, and underbritches. They had sacrificed their shirts to bandage Abercrombie's wound. What would they do when their remaining clothes became tatters?

Lorenzo won the first backgammon game. They started a new game.

"How do you and your wife celebrate Christmas?" Blackie asked.

"We've only been married three months."

"You are missing your first Christmas together. I'm sorry."

"Me too. Eugenie is staying with friends in New Orleans while I'm gone." Lorenzo's thoughts drifted to Louisiana. "Right about now, she is getting ready to go to midnight mass."

"You said your father is a Virginian?"

Lorenzo nodded.

"Were you raised there?"

Lorenzo shook his head. "New Spain."

"How do you come to be in Louisiana?" Sincere interest tinged his voice.

"My father died of consumption three years ago. After his funeral, I left San Antonio and set out for my grandfather's home in Virginia. When I got to New Orleans, I was involved in an altercation and—"

"An altercation?" Blackie gave him a wicked smile. "Isn't that a fancy way of saying you were in a fight?"

"It wasn't my fault."

Blackie laughed heartily. "It never is. All criminals claim they are innocent lambs."

"Do you want to hear the rest of the story or do you want to make fun of me?"

Blackie drummed his fingers over his mouth as if weighing the matter. "Go on with your story."

"As I was saying, I ran into three drunken Brits. They started a fight. To make a long story short, we all ended up in jail. A little later, Don Bernardo released me and made me his ward."

"He took in a street brawler!" Blackie exclaimed. "He was taking quite a chance!"

Lorenzo let the jab pass. "He was repaying an old debt. Years ago, he was badly wounded by the Apaches. My father was his doctor."

"So you've been with Don Bernardo ever since," Blackie concluded.

"No. I served in the Continental Army before coming back to New Orleans."

Blackie grew pensive. "Is that where all the scars came from?"

The question pulled Lorenzo back. For the last week, they had gone shirtless. Apparently, Blackie had wondered about the scars but was too polite to ask about them. Even now, he seemed embarrassed to bring it up.

Eugenie had been surprised on their wedding night to see the crazy quilt of scars hidden by shirts and knee britches.

Lorenzo was surprised by her surprise, then realized she

had never seen him shirtless.

"Dark skin scars very easily," Lorenzo said.

"What about the scar on your back?"

There were several there, but Lorenzo knew which one had intrigued him. "You want to know why I was shot in the back?"

Red-faced, Blackie scratched his head.

Abercrombie, who had been listening in complete disinterest, raised up on an elbow. "You were shot in the back?"

Lorenzo stared into the fire. "I was. I had dressed as an Indian and had gone into a British fort."

"To spy?" Blackie asked.

"To get medicine." Lorenzo told the story, embellishing it, making it more exciting than it was. "When I left the fort and ran to the forest, Saber-Scar shot me in the back."

"Saber-Scar?" Blackie asked.

"His real name was Sergeant Dunstan Andrews. He had a long scar on his cheek. A couple of months after shooting me, he managed to capture me. I got lucky. Friends rescued me. Saber-Scar went to a prisoner-of-war camp, but escaped and tried to kill me. About two years ago, he was hanged for murder." Lorenzo smiled ruefully. "He was a member of an influential British family. The head of the family took exception to his cousin's execution and came to New Orleans for revenge."

"A vendetta," Blackie said. "Fascinating. You're still alive, so one can assume that you killed the other fellow?"

Lorenzo half-smiled. "Don't assume. The cad is still alive. His name is Robert Hawthorne. The next time I run into him,

I'm calling him out for a duel."

"Wouldn't it be wise to simply drop this feud? Live and let live."

"I would be most happy to do so. The Hawthornes have been a thorn in my side for years."

Blackie laughed at Lorenzo's pun.

"Got any more interesting stories, Dr. Bannister?" Abercrombie asked.

Blackie groaned. "Don't encourage him."

Lorenzo ignored him and told about a cattle drive, about Valley Forge, about the time he worked as a spy in Philadelphia.

"You've led an exciting life," Blackie said.

"More exciting than I want," Lorenzo said. "I left the Continental Army and came home to New Orleans to have a normal life. Look at me now."

"A major in the Spanish army who is the adopted son of the Governor of Louisiana," Blackie mumbled, as if he were thinking out loud. "You would make a good hostage. Imagine the ransom someone could get for you. You would be worth your weight in gold."

Lorenzo had never looked at himself that way. It was not a cheery view.

* * *

On Christmas Eve, Gálvez sat in his garden and played a memory game with his step-daughter while he waited for his wife to dress for Midnight Mass. "My ship has come from

Manila," he said, "and it is loaded with silver, gold, and spice."

"My ship has come from Manila," Adelaide said, "and is loaded with silver, gold, spice, and dolls."

"Dolls!" Gálvez exclaimed.

"Yes, *Papacito*. Lots and lots of dolls."

"I see. My ship has come from Manila and is loaded with gold, silver, spice, dolls, and Lorenzo."

"*Papacito*," Adelaide gently scolded. "That's cheating. Uncle Lorenzo isn't a thing."

"I can put anyone or anything I want on my ships." With Havana's permission, he silently added. His mind wandered as he thought about the horse he had given his father-in-law for Christmas. I can get Arabians from our ranch in Spain, but I can't get soldiers from Havana!

Félicité came downstairs wearing a dark blue dress with matching bonnet. "I am ready, *mon coeur*."

"Isn't Eugenie joining us?"

"She does not feel well."

Gálvez knew she was worried about Lorenzo. He was too. The only thing he wanted for Christmas was to see Lorenzo.

Chapter
Twenty-Two

On December 25, 1779, Lorenzo awoke before everyone else and slipped out of the hut, leaving Abercrombie and Blackie asleep on their mats. Christmas Day dawned bright and promising. He took a sip of water from the covered barrel by the doorway and searched the horizon for a ship. Something appeared far in the distance, a mere speck. Hands shading his eyes, Lorenzo followed it.

Blackie emerged, groggy, running a hand through his hair.

Abercrombie followed close behind, stretching and yawning. He went into the bushes to relieve himself.

Blackie poured a dipper of water over his head to wake himself up completely and scrubbed his face with his hands. "Good morning, Lorenzo."

"Do you see that?" Lorenzo asked, his gaze locked on the horizon.

"A ship!" Blackie said in a hopeful voice. "Can you make out its nationality?"

"It looks like it's flying the Union Jack," Lorenzo concluded.

"Drat," said Blackie.

Abercrombie returned from the bushes. He looked due east to the sea. "A ship! I see a ship!" He ran toward the water jumping wildly and waving his arms frantically overhead.

Lorenzo dashed after him. He grabbed his arm.

The lad pulled away and raced off.

Lorenzo broke into a run and tackled him, throwing him face down in the sand.

Abercrombie tried to fight him off. He and Lorenzo wallowed about with Lorenzo trying to pin him down so the ship wouldn't notice them.

"We are rescued!" the lad yelled, anger filling his voice. "Let me up. We have to signal them before they sail off!"

"Stay down!" Lorenzo said. "It's British."

"Oh," he said quietly in sudden understanding. "Do you think they saw us?"

Lorenzo looked up. The ship was dropping anchor. He groaned and smacked his hand repeatedly against the sand. He resisted the urge to punch Abercrombie for betraying them.

* * *

Blackie self-consciously touched the oilskin pouch that protected the Liberty's letter of marque. He recalled Captain Slaughter's instructions. "Keep this on your person. In case of capture, present it to the officer on duty. He is honor-bound to accept it and grant you and the men prisoner-of-war status."

Blackie clenched and unclenched his hands. Honor? The officers on the British ship had no honor. They had ordered their sharpshooters to kill his sailors. A quick vision passed in front of his eyes. Lorenzo, Abercrombie, and he were lined up on the beach, hands raised in surrender, muskets pointed at them. Someone shouted, "Fire."

In the last week, Lorenzo had become like a brother. Without him, he and Abercrombie would not have survived. Neither of them possessed the skills to make it on a deserted island. They had gone twenty-four hours without food and water when they heard someone singing. They followed the sound and found Lorenzo.

Rubbing the heel of his hand over his forehead, Blackie made his decision. He walked inside the hut, dropped to his knees, and dug a hole in the sand. He placed the oilskin pouch inside, but paused. For a moment, he stared at it.

An immense sadness swept over him. Captain Slaughter had given it to him, saying that every good sailor wore an oilskin pouch to protect important papers. By burying it, he was severing his last link to the captain. Blackie filled in the hole and smoothed sand over it to hide the fact that something was buried there. He placed a sleep mat over it.

The Stars and Stripes had not protected his men when they were in the water. The letter of marque would not protect Lorenzo and Abercrombie. A plan formed in his mind. He bowed his head and asked God to help him play the role that would save them all.

Lorenzo watched the British prepare the longboat. He considered hiding in the jungle, but rejected the idea. The British would only come after them. Trying to fight the British off with spears and arrows was suicide.

The British launched the longboat. Lorenzo counted thirteen sailors, most armed with muskets.

Blackie stepped to Lorenzo's side.

Eyes narrowed in deep thought, Blackie stood with his hands laced behind him. "Gentemen, I am a shipwrecked English nobleman. Lorenzo, you are my servant. Abercrombie, you are a cabin boy from the . . ." His voice faltered.

"The Primrose." Lorenzo said the first name that popped into mind. He understood what Blackie was doing. He was making up a story to tell the British.

"The Primrose," Blackie repeated. "We were traveling on a private merchant vessel bound for Mobile when a storm came up unexpectedly. It sank the ship. I was cast upon this miserable shore with a servant and a cabin boy. We have lived here for the last week." He turned his head toward Lorenzo. "As my servant, you do not speak without my permission. If someone asks you a question, look at me. I will answer for you. Obey my orders without hesitation. Servants never look their superiors straight in the eye."

Lorenzo lowered his gaze. "By your command."

"No. You say 'Yes, master' or 'No, master.'"

"Yes, master."

"Excellent." Blackie stood a little straighter, as if gathering his courage. He walked down to the water's edge and waved his hands overhead to hail the approaching longboat.

While Abercrombie hovered around the fire pit, Lorenzo joined Blackie, staying slightly behind him like a good servant. "This is where your English accent comes in handy," Lorenzo whispered.

"Quite so." One side of Blackie's mouth curled into a smile. "Follow my lead, Lowell."

"Lorenzo." The correction came without thinking.

Blackie shook his head and scowled. "A servant never talks back. It is bad form. It is even worse to correct the master."

Lorenzo felt like giving himself a boot in the rump. If he was a servant, he had to start thinking like one.

When the longboat was within earshot, Blackie put on his most charming smile. "God be praised! We are rescued."

Several British sailors leaped from the boat and left it in the care of their companions. They leveled pistols and muskets that targeted the three of them.

"What is the meaning of this?" Blackie demanded, standing with his legs astraddle, fists on hips. "We saw Spanish ships pass by and did not hail them, expecting rude behavior from them. I expected better from Englishmen!"

"You saw Spanish ships?" asked the senior officer of the landing party, a horse-faced man who wore a long mane of hair tied at the nape of his neck.

"Indeed we did. Several, sailing south. I decided it was better to stay on the island than to fall in with them."

"Search them," Horse-Face ordered.

"Search us?" Blackie asked. "Look at us, gentlemen." He held his arms out to his side. "Our clothes hang by threads! Where are we going to hide weapons?"

Horse-Face reddened.

"Outrageous!" Blackie exclaimed. "To entertain the notion of a search of my person. I am the son of Sir Edmund, Earl of Somersby, a peer of the realm. My father sits in the House of Lords and I daresay he will be more than a bit upset to learn that you have treated me like a common criminal!"

"Christ's blood, Mister Sedwick," a sour-looking sailor said to the man in charge, "but that man's a diego." He pointed at Lorenzo.

"Don't be ridiculous!" Blackie snapped. "Do you think I would associate with a damned Spaniard?" He said the last word as if it were dirty. "That is Lowell, my gentleman's gentleman."

"I've seen you somewhere before," the man said, studying Lorenzo from head to toe.

Trying to look stupid and unconcerned, Lorenzo lowered his gaze. If he had met this fellow before, he had probably been in uniform. It always changed the way a man looked.

Blackie pursed his lips in annoyance. "As I was saying, my father will pay a generous reward to anyone who delivers me safely into his hands."

"And him?"

Blackie rolled his eyes. "Of course." He paused. A look of

amusement surfaced. "Although I rather doubt that Father will ransom him at the terribly exorbitant rate he will pay for me."

Smooth though Blackie was in his lies, Mister Sedwick remained unconvinced. "Where does your father have an estate?"

"Estates," Blackie corrected. "There's one in London, on the outskirts, of course. The city is an absolute cesspit in the summer. Then, there is the castle in Scotland on Loch Lomond. We have a couple of smaller summer homes in—"

"That will do," the man snarled. "What happened to him?" He indicated Abercrombie.

Lorenzo's insides collapsed. How did they account for the lad's gunshot wound?

"Unfortunate encounter with a jellyfish." Blackie wrinkled his nose. "Nasty wound. I treated it as best I could. I am a physician, but I have never treated a jellyfish wound before."

Lorenzo kept his face expressionless to hide his admiration for Blackie's quick thinking. It was a bold move and was the best response possible.

Mr. Sedwick, the horse-faced man, addressed his sailors. "Help the little lord to the longboat."

"M'lord," Lorenzo said, recalling his father's medical bag, "may I go for our things?"

"Ah, yes. Excellent point."

"Make haste," Mister Sedwick said, "or we shall leave you behind."

Lorenzo dashed to the hut, picked up his father's medical

bag and the amputation kit.

A few minutes later, they shoved off and left Cozumel behind. Lorenzo could not help shivering as they headed toward the British ship. Once onboard, there was no escape should Blackie's ruse go sour.

Chapter
Twenty-Three

Something is finally working out right, Lorenzo thought as he stretched out on a bunk and stared at the ceiling. The goose-feather mattress beneath him was an improvement over his mat in the hut. Two officers had relinquished their room so Blackie and Lorenzo could have a place to stay. The quarters were cramped, but at least they were no longer on the island. Lorenzo and Blackie were better off than Abercrombie. He had a hammock strung between two hooks on the gun deck.

An officer about Lorenzo's size had given him clean clothes. If the winds were favorable, they would dock in Mobile by late afternoon.

Lorenzo laced his hands behind his head and waited for his turn to clean up before the noonday meal in the captain's cabin.

Blackie hummed a hymn while he whisked shaving lather in

a mug. He complained that Lorenzo sang while he worked, but did not seem to realize that he did the same thing. After a week with a Methodist, Lorenzo knew several hymns by heart: *O For a Thousand Tongues to Sing, The Doxology, Hark! The Herald Angels Sing, Am I a Soldier of the Cross.*

From this angle, Lorenzo could see Blackie's face and his reflection in the mirror. It made him think about his mental problem. Like the reflection in the mirror, there was a man named "Blackie" who was only a reflection of the original. One of them had lived for twenty or so years, the other but eight months.

Blackie would be adrift without the captain watching out for him. Lorenzo felt it was time to broach the subject of his mental condition. He cleared his throat. "Remember when you said that Cozumel would be a lovely place to live?"

"I do not recollect saying that."

"You did."

"If that is the case, I take it back."

The room fell silent. Beyond the walls, the sea slapped against the hull.

"I've been thinking," Lorenzo said.

"What now?" Blackie asked.

"That jellyfish remark was clever."

"I have my moments."

"Did you ever consider that you told the truth back there? Maybe you are a physician."

Razor poised near one cheek, Blackie slowly turned. "What

are you blathering about?"

"Nothing. Forget I said anything."

"No, you said something. What did you say?"

Lorenzo swung his legs over the bunk. "Captain Slaughter told me about your condition."

Blackie frowned. He turned to the mirror and finished shaving. As usual, he remained the picture of absolute calm, although Lorenzo suspected a thousand thoughts were galloping through his head.

Blackie wiped away leftover lather with a towel. "What did the captain tell you?"

"That you have lost your memory."

"Why did he tell you that?"

"I'm not sure. It came up in the conversation one day."

"I see," Blackie said in an unruffled voice. "You knew but said nothing?"

"What was there to say?"

"Sharing an island with a madman must have been uncomfortable for you."

"It certainly was, but Abercrombie can't help it if he is a little slow at times."

For several seconds, Blackie blinked at Lorenzo before he caught the joke. "I must say you have the strangest sense of humor."

"So I've been told," Lorenzo said. "What will you do when we get to Mobile?"

"Get out of town posthaste."

"Where will you head?"

"I have no clue."

"What will you do for a living?"

"Again, no clue. If I can find a ship that needs a quartermaster, I'll sign on."

"That seems a waste of talent," Lorenzo said, choosing his words wisely. "You should practice medicine."

Blackie looked at him in consternation. "Don't be ridiculous."

"I am convinced that you are a trained physician. You finished the amputation for me. You took care of Abercrombie's gunshot wound. I could not have done better. You have a natural talent for medicine. You could set up a practice in New Orleans."

"Who would want me as a physician? I don't even know my name."

"Dr. Black has a nice ring to it."

"How do I prove I have credentials?"

"My father graduated from medical school in Edinburgh. Based on your accent, you probably did too."

"But not under the name 'Black.'"

"It doesn't matter what name is on your diploma. The important thing is that you are a trained physician. All you need is a sworn statement from two doctors saying that you are qualified to practice medicine. Based on their recommendation, the city council of New Orleans will issue a license."

Blackie rubbed his hand up and down the side of his face.

Lorenzo could tell he was almost convinced and plunged on. "You have a God-given talent for medicine." The word 'talent' made a story come to mind. "Do you remember the three servants in the Bible who were given talents?"

"Yes, Matthew, Chapter 25."

"I'll take your word on that. The point is that you should not waste your talents."

"That was a parable about money."

"But the principle remains the same. Do not waste what God has given you."

"Physician, heal thyself," Blackie said, giving him a significant look.

"What does that mean?"

"Are you Major Bannister or Doctor Bannister?"

"I plan to set up a medical practice in New Orleans when the war is over. I'll need a partner. Bannister and Black has a nice ring to it."

"Black and Bannister would sound even better."

Lorenzo laughed. "My name comes first in the alphabet."

"I could change mine to Abercrombie."

"Abercrombie and Bannister will not fit on a shingle."

"Bannister and Black." Blackie leaned over the basin and splashed water on his face. He toweled himself dry. "Do I have a first name?"

"My father's name was Jack."

"Jack Black? I don't think so."

"Abercrombie Black?" Lorenzo suggested.

Blackie opened his mouth slightly. "Surely you jest."

"I jest."

"You are as mad as the proverbial March hare."

"Physician, heal thyself."

Blackie blew out a long sigh of exasperation. "How does your wife tolerate you?"

Lorenzo merely smiled.

Chapter
Twenty-Four

Freedom drew closer and closer. Lorenzo rested his forearms on the ship's railing and tried to curb his excitement. The sooner he and his companions were off the ship, the better. Setting foot on English soil was far from appealing, not to mention dangerous, but once ashore, he could get a horse and travel overland to Louisiana.

Blackie joined him at the ship's railing.

"We seem to be slowing down," Lorenzo said.

"These are tricky waters." Blackie pointed to a sandbar barely poking its head above water. "The captain does not want to go aground."

"What happens if your ship gets stuck?" Lorenzo asked.

"I would not know. I have never been that incompetent."

Dauphin Island slid by on the left, Mobile Point on the right.

The ship headed north in Mobile Bay, gliding past fat cows grazing in green pastures.

"Nice cows," Blackie remarked.

Lorenzo tried not to laugh, but failed. He sputtered.

"Did I say something humorous?" Blackie cast him a strange look.

Lorenzo glanced about to make sure no one could overhear them. "Those cows will be Mobile's downfall."

"How so?"

"I'll explain later."

"Explain now."

"Those cows feed the British at Pensacola. So do those fields." Lorenzo nodded toward acre after acre lying in fallow. "Take away Mobile and you take away the capital's main food supply. When the general was drawing up battle plans, he wavered between Mobile and Pensacola. Which should he attack? Those cows tipped the scales. He decided all that beef was better off in Spanish stomachs."

Blackie's voice dropped to a whisper. "Mobile's fate rests on a herd of cows?"

Lorenzo nodded.

Mobile Bay turned into Mobile River. The first building to come into view was Fort Charlotte, a brick-and-stone structure at water level. It covered eleven acres and was the second most formidable fort in the Gulf. Only Veracruz surpassed it.

Lorenzo stood in awe of Fort Charlotte. On paper, it hadn't looked so grand and imposing.

Maybe, Lorenzo thought, the general is making a huge mistake by attacking it. Maybe he should go after Pensacola.

In front of the fort was marshland. Behind it, to the north, Mobile faded into dense forest. The town extended about half a mile on the level plain above the river. Most houses were one story, made of brick, with large courtyards. They appeared to be vacant. A few were in good shape and well tended. Mobile had about five hundred residents. To judge by the number of uniforms Lorenzo saw, most of them were soldiers.

The ship approached a wooden wharf about a hundred feet long that ran from the fort to the river. It was the only dock that connected the town to ships sailing the river.

Abercrombie approached carrying his burlap bag. He deposited it beside Lorenzo's medical bag and amputation kit. "I have to talk to a man. Says he knows of a ship bound for Boston."

"Make haste," Blackie said. "We want to get off the minute we dock."

"I'll be right back," Abercrombie promised.

Ten more minutes, Lorenzo said to himself, and we will be ashore. Ten more minutes and we are out of jeopardy.

* * *

"Ten bottles of rum are waiting for me at the dram shop," Hawthorne said, handing Davy Morgan twenty pounds that he promptly crammed into his jacket pocket next to his flick-knife. "Stop at the king's bakery—"

"It closed an hour ago," Davy said.

"Of course, it did," Hawthorne said, "simply to spite me!" He slung his hands in agitation. "Guests will be here in three hours. Why did Mrs. Welch pick today to have a baby?"

"Just to spite you, sir," Davy said with mock seriousness. "The Prince of Wales is pulling in. I could buy something there."

"It will take hours to unload!"

"Um, sir," Davy said, shifting uncomfortably from foot to foot. "I wasn't planning to go through regular channels."

"Are you suggesting I serve smuggled goods?"

"Sure," Davy said. "Why not?"

Tonight, the guest list consisted of the Anglican vicar, the fort's commander, and its surgeon. Davy had never seen anyone who enjoyed entertaining more than Colonel Hawthorne. He thrived on parties and had become famous for them. At first, Davy had worried that Hawthorne's constant carousing would delay his recovery. It actually seemed to hasten it.

"Um, sir," Davy said, "there's a man onboard who always—"

Hawthorne put his hands over his ears. "Aaaahhhhh! I am an officer of the court. I am not listening." He lowered his hands. "Are you still here? Don't you have some nefarious deed to do?"

"That depends. If I get in trouble, will you be my barrister?"

"I do not work pro bono."

"What does that mean?"

"Pro bono. For the common good. In other words, free."

Davy stored the word away for later use. That was what he liked most about working for Colonel Hawthorne. He learned all kinds of information, some of it useful, some of it merely interesting. "The wharf can be a dangerous place. I could run into trouble. Perhaps I should not go." He made a pretense of taking off his jacket.

Before he had one arm out of a sleeve, Hawthorne grabbed him and propelled him toward the door. "Do what you must and be quick about it. Should you be arrested, I will bail you out."

Davy was sure that Hawthorne would do it, too. The colonel knew everyone in town, and everyone in town liked him. Because there was no courthouse in Mobile, legal proceedings were held at Hawthorne's house. Hawthorne served as a civil magistrate.

Davy turned to go. At his back, he heard the colonel say, "Be careful, son."

Davy always carried a flick-knife. He used it for such heinous activities as cutting string, opening the mail, and cleaning his fingernails. He had never used it to defend himself, but it was a comfort to have it handy. When a ship pulled in, sailors came ashore and the complexion of Mobile changed. It was not a change for the better.

As Davy walked down Conti Street, he heard a woman call for her children in French. A Scottish tune filtered from an open window across the street as someone sang about a "bonny lass." Further on, an Irish accent threatened a mule with bodily harm if it did not move. Davy made a right on Royal and nearly collided with Manchac, a slave who belonged to one of the British officers assigned to the fort.

They greeted each other and continued on their way.

Davy melted into the shadows cast by Fort Charlotte. His

eyes raked the sailors unloading the ship as he searched for a smuggler named Sedwick.

*   *   *

Lorenzo stood with Blackie near the gangway and waited for Abercrombie. He kept an eye on two men standing nearby.

The sailor who had been suspicious of Lorenzo and called him a diego was talking to Mr. Sedwick, the horse-faced officer. A man with pasty skin and hard-set lips beneath a black moustache walked up the gangway and joined them. He wore a jacket with large gilt buttons, a scarlet waistcoat, and a sword at his side. The stranger's eyes made Lorenzo's blood run cold. Dark and deeply set, they were the eyes of an assassin. The man suddenly looked at Lorenzo, giving him the impression that he had become the topic of conversation.

Lorenzo had a bad feeling about him. Lowering his gaze, he half-turned, but kept the man in his peripheral vision and looked for an escape route. There was none, short of jumping over the side. To get off the ship, they would have to walk past him. Lorenzo scanned the wharf. It was a bustling scene crowded with men, some unloading the ship, some welcoming friends, still others loitering about.

Lorenzo wished he had a weapon. His father's medical bag, the amputation kit, and Abercrombie's burlap bag rested at his feet. In the last week, he had ruined all the surgical instruments in the kit by cutting firewood and opening coconuts. He had lost the long knife in an unfortunate accident while swimming in the reef.

Servants, slaves, and sailors filled the deck, making it a jumble of noise and a confusion of people.

Lorenzo resigned himself to walking past the knot of men watching him. He prayed that he, Blackie, and Abercrombie could become lost in the crowd.

*　*　*

Davy waited in the shadows of Fort Charlotte at the spot where he usually met the smuggler and watched men go up and down the gangway carrying casks and crates on their shoulders. Once in a while, two men carried a large object between them.

A figure on the main deck caught his eye. He looked familiar. Davy strained to see him and walked toward the ship to get a better look. He stopped halfway there. Recognition burst upon him. It was Major Bannister! Davy had played the fife at his wedding. He started to lift his hand to wave hello, but caught himself. What was a Spanish officer doing on a British ship? Why was he out of uniform? There was only one reason Davy could think of. He was a spy.

Conflicting emotions struggled through Davy. On one hand, he was proud of being British and was loyal through and through to King George. On the other hand, there was Eugenie to consider. He barely knew the man she had married, but he knew her well. She was a dear friend. Friend? No. Eugenie was more than that. Davy loved her. His ears burned with embarrassment to admit the truth. He coveted Major Bannister's wife.

Instinct told him the major was in trouble. Davy did not give a whit about the man, but a sense of loyalty to Eugenie urged him on. He headed up the gangway, pushing past men who growled at him and spat out curses that he ignored. At the top, he stepped on deck and looked about. Seeing no one paying attention to him, he walked toward the main mast, keeping an eye on Bannister. Davy shoved his hands in his jacket pocket and strolled toward the railing as if he hadn't a care in the world. He could tell that the major had spotted him.

He tilted his head questioningly as if asking a silent question. *Are you going to betray me?*

While pondering what to do, Davy noticed the man standing beside the major. He had dark blue eyes, brown hair, and pale English skin. At that second, he spoke to Major Bannister and flashed a self-assured smile. He radiated goodness and kindness.

Davy's mouth went dry. He had never met the man. Of that, he was certain. But he knew who he was. He had seen that self-assured smile on the portrait that he had retrieved from Baton Rouge. The man was Colonel Hawthorne's dead brother.

Chapter Twenty-Five

Davy veered away from Major Bannister. The man's eyes followed him in doubt and questioning as he walked to the railing three feet away. He had to think about this unexpected development. Could he be wrong? He had once heard that everyone had an exact double somewhere. The man with Major Bannister and the man in the portrait could be twins.

The major rested his elbows on the railing, his back to the sun sinking below the fringe of tall trees behind the fort.

Davy waited for the major to turn toward him and say something, but he stubbornly insisted upon watching a cluster of men by the gangplank. Davy scanned them and understood his concern. They looked dangerous.

Davy leaned over the railing and twisted his head left and right as if searching for something on the wharf. "Are you in trouble?" he asked out of the corner of his mouth.

"Yes," Major Bannister hissed, his lips barely moving.

"Who is the man with you?"

"A friend."

"What's his name?"

"Dr. Black."

The name gave Davy pause. It was not what he expected. "An alias?" he asked after a long moment.

Bannister gave a barely perceptible nod.

Then it could be Evan Hawthorne. Why was he with Major Bannister? Why was he using an alias?

Davy glanced over his shoulder at the three men by the gangway and then looked toward the fort. "How can I help?"

Bannister's eyes slid sideways as if judging the sincerity of the offer. He laced his hands together and flexed them in front of himself. He yawned and pretended to be bored. "I need a weapon."

Davy reached into his pocket. His fingers closed around the twenty pounds the colonel had given him and the handle of the flick-knife. He inched toward Lorenzo, bent down, took off his shoe, and turned it upside down as if dumping a pebble from it. He squatted and put the shoe back on. He used the opportunity to slip the flick-knife from his pocket and hide it behind the major's leather bag. He straightened and moved away.

Bannister continued to stare at the men by the gangway. He appeared to be humming, still maintaining a bored look.

* * *

Josiah Crowe rolled cask after cask from the back of the ship's hold to the stairs where he turned them over to sailors. They, in turn, carried the casks up the stairs.

I am a navigator, Josiah thought, but here I am—reduced to a common sailor! The next time he saw Augustus Fitzgibbons, he would give the man a piece of his mind. Putting him on a pirate ship! Suffering the indignity of being imprisoned by the Spanish! And now, working like a negro! Augustus had promised him a wad of money once the chest was found. No amount could repay the humiliations he had suffered.

"Last one," the foreman said. "Let's go topside, Crowe."

Josiah slowly climbed toward daylight.

* * *

Trying to act casual, Lorenzo bent over and picked up the flick-knife. He hid it in the palm of his hand.

A shadow of worry passed over Blackie's face. "What are you doing?"

"Where is Abercrombie?" Lorenzo asked.

As if on cue, the lad came from below decks.

"There he is," Blackie said. He signaled for Abercrombie to join them at the gangway. "Let's go, Lowell."

Two things happened at the same time. Abercrombie walked toward them. A man emerged from the hold carrying a cask.

Inwardly, Lorenzo groaned.

Josiah Crowe stopped. He looked straight at Blackie. His mouth fell open.

"Let's go, Lowell!" Blackie said, nudging Lorenzo forward. He looked at him curiously, apparently not realizing that they had been discovered.

Josiah Crowe put the cask down. He hurried over to the

179

knot of men waiting by the gangway and spoke to them. He pointed to Blackie.

"We are in big trouble," Lorenzo said. "Look over there."

Blackie looked in the direction of Lorenzo's gaze. "It cannot be . . . My luck cannot be that bad!"

Abercrombie stopped in his tracks. He stepped behind a bank of sailors. Apparently, he had seen Josiah Crowe too and knew that the man's presence was not good news.

Josiah and the three men strode forward.

"That one," Josiah said, pointing to Blackie, "is a pirate named Blackie. The other fellow is a Spanish officer from the San Juan Nepomuceno."

"What kind of tomfoolery is this?" Blackie snorted. "I am not a pirate."

"He's lying!"

"The man is mad as a March hare. Begone!"

"We've caught big fish!" Josiah exclaimed in a victorious tone. His gaze burned a path to Lorenzo. "That fellow . . . He happens to be Major Lorenzo Bannister of the Louisiana Regiment. He is a staff officer for none other than General Bernardo de Gálvez himself."

Everyone within hearing stopped what they were doing. They crowded around.

Blackie looked disdainfully at Mr. Sedwick, the horse-faced officer. "The man is a raving lunatic. Get him out of my sight."

"Is he really now?" The question came from the dark-eyed man. "Hello," he said, directing his attention to Lorenzo. "It has been a long time."

"Do I know you?"

"How soon they forget. Augustus Fitzgibbons. Philadelphia. The winter of 1778. We met at Sir William's house."

"Sir William?" Lorenzo asked. "I don't know anyone by that name." It was a lie. The name took Lorenzo back to a spying expedition for General Washington. He had indeed met General Sir William Howe . . . and Augustus Fitzgibbons.

"I never forget a face. Never. In the name of the king," Fitzgibbons said in a victorious voice, "you are under arrest. Guards!"

Two marines watching the unloading of the hold pushed their way through the crowd. They forced Lorenzo's hands behind his back and slapped on irons. Morgan's flick-knife clattered to the deck.

"Take them to Fort Charlotte," the dark-eyed man said. "I shall dispose of them directly."

*   *   *

Davy Morgan's head was spinning. He watched the arrest unfold in a mixture of horror and disbelief. After hearing the British accent from the man called "Blackie," Davy was convinced he was Evan Hawthorne.

Colonel Hawthorne's brother was under arrest for piracy. Major Bannister, for espionage. Both were hanging offenses.

*   *   *

The guard took off Lorenzo's irons and gave him a spiteful push into a cell.

Blackie stumbled in after him.

The door slammed shut, the key ground in the lock, and the guards turned and left.

"I had hoped for better accommodations," Blackie said, looking around in disappointment.

Their cell in Fort Charlotte was little more than four feet wide by three feet long and had a dirt floor, no windows, no furniture, nothing but a chamber pot. Three sides of the cell were brick. The fourth consisted of a wooden grating with open squares about four inches by four inches.

Lorenzo slid to the floor and leaned his head against the brick wall.

After several moments, Blackie joined him. "I am sincerely sorry. This is all my fault."

"How do you figure that?" Lorenzo asked.

"If I had not gone to the San Juan Nepomuceno looking for a surgeon . . ." His voice trailed.

Lorenzo smiled and shook his head. "Don't blame yourself. If I had stayed on the San Juan Nepomuceno—"

"That would have been completely out of character. You did the right thing. It just did not work out right." He paused. "Do you perchance have an escape plan?"

"No."

Blackie sighed. "Hope springs eternal."

"I'm open to suggestions," Lorenzo said.

"Sorry. I'm fresh out."

"What does King George do to pirates?" Lorenzo asked.

"He hangs them. It's something I needn't worry about as I am a privateer and not a pirate."

Lorenzo chuckled softly.

"It looks like Abercrombie got away," Blackie said.

"I'm glad."

The conversation lapsed. Lorenzo searched for a way to keep it alive. Talking took his mind off his misery. A stench of urine clung to the cell walls. The only light came from a crack under the main door and it was slowly fading. Lorenzo knew they would soon be plunged into total darkness.

The door burst open. Two soldiers entered, one carrying a lantern that sent shadows leaping around the room.

"The judge said he wants to see Bannister first."

"Which one's he?"

"Damned if I know. Which one looks like his luck just ran out?"

"Bannister?" a soldier said, looking at Blackie.

"Over here," Lorenzo said, lifting a hand.

"All right, Bannister," the guard said, putting a key in the door and turning it. "Move sharp now. Judge doesn't like to be kept waiting."

"English justice moves faster than Spanish justice," Lorenzo said, rising.

"So it would appear," Blackie said, rising as well. He offered his hand. "It was a pleasure."

Lorenzo's mind went blank. He could not think of a sensible thing to say as he shook Blackie's hand.

Chapter Twenty-Six

Two armed guards led Lorenzo through a heavy wooden gate in the fort's northern wall past houses in various states of disrepair. They made a left and stopped in front of a rusty gate that screeched when a guard pushed on it. A dirt path led to the most elegant house on the block, a one-story brick surrounded by lush gardens.

Someone, Lorenzo noted, had spent a lot of time tending to the magnolias, wax myrtles, and English roses. A wooden bench and a small table sat in their midst. He assumed this was the judge's residence. A town the size of Mobile was too small to have a courthouse.

The guards knocked on the door and waited for an answer.

"Come!" someone called from inside.

A guard opened the door and signaled for Lorenzo to go inside.

He entered a room ablaze in lights.

Robert Hawthorne sat at a table, writing. He wore a black

robe and a curled white wig. He glanced up, put a quill pen in its holder and rocked an ink blotter over a piece of parchment. "Wait outside," he told the guards.

They dutifully obeyed, closing the door behind them.

"You?" Lorenzo asked, perplexed. "You are the judge?"

"Rather ironic, don't you think? When last we met, you held my life in your hands. Now, our roles are reversed." He nodded toward a chair across from him.

Lorenzo understood that he was to sit. He took in his surroundings in one fell swoop. In one corner, a grandfather clock droned out the hour. A sideboard held a silver tray and several decanters filled with liquids of various hues. Oddly, the wall above the fireplace was covered with a sheet.

Hawthorne leaned forward, hands laced together, resting on the table. "How have you been, Dr. Bannister?"

"Fine. You are looking well. It appears you have made a complete recovery."

"I had an excellent doctor."

Lorenzo inclined his head slightly to acknowledge the compliment.

"You have been charged with espionage. In spite of the bad blood between us, I do not wish to see you swing." Hawthorne offered him a half-smile. "I can see the wheels and cogs turning in your head. You are asking yourself why I care about your fate." His smile turned bitter. "The sad truth is . . . I care not one iota. I do, however, care very much about the fate of your cellmate."

"Blackie?" Lorenzo asked, confused.

"Evan."

"You know him?"

"I know him very well." Hawthorne picked up a lit candlestick and walked to the sheet-covered wall. He pulled off the drape.

"*Dios mío*," Lorenzo muttered, rising and taking a step toward the portrait. "That's Blackie."

"No, that's my brother, Evan."

Lorenzo pivoted toward Hawthorne. He stood in stunned silence. It took a moment to find his tongue. "Blackie is your brother?"

"Evan," Hawthorne corrected. "His name is Evan Hawthorne. I want to know everything, starting with how you and my brother met."

"Why don't you ask him yourself?"

"When Davy told me that he had found my brother, my first impulse was to dash to the jail to see him, but Davy stopped me. He said Evan was using an alias. When he told me that Evan was with you and you were out of uniform, I knew something was wrong. That's why I asked to see you before Evan. I decided to proceed with caution."

"Because?" Lorenzo prompted.

"Because everyone thinks Evan is dead. Perhaps we should not disabuse anyone of that notion. My brother was the garrison surgeon at Baton Rouge."

Lorenzo winced. A British officer serving on an American privateer was guilty of treason, a hanging offense.

"I have to save my brother," Hawthorne said. He covered the

portrait again. "But I need information. Tell me everything you know."

Before Lorenzo could begin, Davy Morgan came into the room carrying Lorenzo's medical bags. "You left these on the ship. I thought you would want them."

"Yes, thank you!"

Davy set them down. "What did I miss, sir?"

"Dr. Bannister was about to explain my brother's erratic behavior."

Lorenzo told them about pirates coming aboard the San Juan Nepomuceno and asking for medical aid. How he volunteered to help them. About amputating the captain's leg. The storm blowing the ship off course. Being attacked by the British. The shipwreck on Cozumel. Their arrest and imprisonment. He left out the part about Blackie burying a chest on Isla Mujeres.

Both Morgan and Hawthorne showed keen interest in the story.

"There is something you should know about your brother," Lorenzo said. "He has no memory of events before April of this year."

"April," Hawthorne said. He and Davy exchanged significant looks.

"Is there a special significance to April?" Lorenzo asked.

Hawthorne nodded. He went to the sideboard, opened a drawer, took out a small book and handed it to Lorenzo. "This is Evan's diary."

Lorenzo poured over it, absorbing each page. "*Válgame*," he whispered when he reached the end. "The captain was right."

"The captain?" Davy asked.

"Captain Slaughter. The Liberty's captain. He met Blackie by chance and offered him a position as quartermaster. He suspected that Blackie . . . Evan had been through something that made his mind slam shut. Now I understand why he lost his memory and became Blackie. In a manner of speaking, your brother Evan died along with his family and Blackie the pirate was born."

Hawthorne pondered that. "Be that as it may, if they hang Blackie, it will go very badly for Evan." He scratched his head as if trying to solve a big problem. Frowning at the covered painting, he counted the charges against his brother. "Piracy. Desertion. Treason. Any of those are hanging offenses." Hawthorne locked gazes with Lorenzo. "I am not going to let my brother hang."

"I certainly hope not. I plan to open a medical practice with him in New Orleans."

Hawthorne looked surprised by the announcement.

Lorenzo gave him a lopsided grin. "Of course, that was before I knew he was your brother."

"And now?"

"He is a talented physician. It would be an honor to practice medicine with him. Tell me about your brother. What was Evan like?"

Hawthorne paused and his eyes took on a faraway look, as if trying to decide where to begin. "He was the second born, four years younger than I. At age twelve, he went to the university."

"Isn't that rather young?"

"Evan was a genius. He was also the tenderhearted one. Whenever an animal was hurt, it was brought to Evan. He worked miracles. Once, he raised a baby robin. No one thought it would live. Through his tender care, it grew strong enough to fly away. Another time, a tenant cut into a bed of baby mice. Evan saw the man prepare to kill them and intervened. He raised the mice." Hawthorne smiled as if at a fond memory. "When time came to let them go, he released them on a neighboring estate."

Lorenzo chuckled.

"There was a squirrel with two broken legs and a pigeon with a broken wing. I could go on and on. It was natural that he would go to the University of Edinburgh and study medicine."

"So I was right!" Lorenzo exclaimed. "He is a doctor."

"And quite a good one. He visited the colonies and that was his undoing. He was traveling with a naturalist who was studying the flora and fauna of the Floridas. He met a woman in Natchez named Josephine. He was smitten. The man had survived twenty-three years as a bachelor. He gave up a good position at a hospital in London to settle permanently in the colonies. By then, the little squabble with the colonies had begun. He joined the army as a doctor posted to Baton Rouge. He bought a plantation and moved his wife and child from Natchez. Then, suddenly, letters from Evan stopped. It was not like him at all. I did not know what had happened until Major Calderón gave me the diary."

"How did he get it?"

"My brother's plantation was confiscated when the Spanish took over. To Major Calderón's credit, he gave me personal items that belonged to Evan and his family." He waved vaguely toward the portrait.

"What do we do, Dr. Bannister?" Morgan asked. "How do we break it to him gently? How do we tell him who he is?"

Lorenzo ran his hands through his hair. "I don't know. Maybe we don't. Right now, he is fully functional. It is very odd. He cannot remember personal memories, but he can remember how to do surgery. Maybe he is better off not remembering." Lorenzo tapped the diary's cover. "Perhaps it would be cruel to help him remember that."

Hawthorne looked concerned. "If we told him, do you think we would do more harm than good?"

"That's possible. I've been around him, observing him, and I don't know what to advise. We know very little about how the mind works. Maybe, in time, his memory will come back on its own."

"But he was a doctor," Morgan said, "and was around death all the time. Why did his mind go away?"

"I can tell you from personal experience," Lorenzo said, "that it is different when the patient is someone you love. You feel helpless, useless, angry." He thought back to the awful days of sitting by his father's bedside while he wasted away from consumption. His death had scarred Lorenzo forever.

Lorenzo slapped his forehead in a sudden burst of remembrance.

"What?" Hawthorne asked.

"While we were on the island, we had a lot of free time to talk. I told your brother about your cousin Dunstan, about what you did last summer and how you attempted to avenge Dunstan's death. I told him everything."

"Marvelous. I've been slandered to my own brother."

"Stop thinking like a lawyer and listen to what I just said. I went into glorious detail about your family. I named you. I described you. There was not a glimmer of recognition. I think you could walk up to him and he would look at you as if you were a complete stranger."

Lorenzo instantly regretted his statement when a pained expression flickered across Hawthorne's face.

"I'm sorry to be so blunt," Lorenzo said, "but I think you need to recognize the fact that he may never know who you are."

"That doesn't alter the fact that I know who he is. We must save him. Any suggestions?"

Lorenzo thought about that. "Congress gave Captain Slaughter a letter of marque. That makes Blackie a prisoner of war. He can be exchanged for a British sailor."

"Where is it now?"

"I don't know. It was probably lost when the Liberty sank. I can give a sworn statement that I saw it."

Hawthorne smiled ruefully. "The letter of marque that will hang Dr. Evan Hawthorne will save a pirate named Blackie. Life is full of little ironies." He paused. "Does it cover an officer in an army allied with the United States?"

Lorenzo could tell he was thinking out loud. "I was out of uniform. That translates as 'spy.'"

"No. It is reasonable for a castaway to be out of uniform." Hawthorne brightened. "General Gálvez must have a couple of prisoners of war in New Orleans left over from the Battle of Baton Rouge."

"Yes! I see where you are going with this."

Hawthorne dug through a pile of papers on his desk. "I know I have one here somewhere. Davy! Where is that blasted parole paper?"

Davy pulled it from a folder and handed it to Hawthorne who bent over it and filled in blanks. He looked over it, his lips moving slightly as he read. "That should do the trick!"

Lorenzo studied the paper. It read:

PAROLE FOR PRISONER EXCHANGE

I, Lorenzo Bannister, Medical Physician, hereby acknowledge to have been made Prisoner of War by Colonel Robert Hawthorne, and have been permitted by Colonel Durnford, Commanding Officer of Fort Charlotte, to return to New Orleans or any part of Louisiana in order to procure an exchange for a person of my rank.

If not executed, I do hereby promise and engage on my most Sacred Word of Honor to deliver myself up a prisoner to said Colonel Durnford or the officer commanding at Fort Charlotte within the space of forty days from the date hereof.

I also promise on my sacred Honor not to say, do or cause to be said or done, anything to the prejudice of Great Britain or give any intelligence to the Enemies thereof, but in all things behave myself agreeable to this obligation.

In witness whereof I hereunto set my hand this Twenty-Seventh day of December 1779.

"Are the terms acceptable?"

"Yes. Will Colonel Durnford agree to this?"

Hawthorne's amusement at Lorenzo's question was evident.

"Did I say something funny?"

"Before your unexpected arrival, I planned to entertain guests. One of them was Colonel Durnford. He is quite an agreeable fellow." Hawthorne handed Lorenzo a quill. "Sign here." He pointed to the appropriate place.

"What about Blackie?" Lorenzo asked, pen poised over paper. "I will not leave him behind."

"Entirely understandable." Hawthorne pulled a second document from the folder and began to write. "Davy, prepare the portable desk." His attention shifted to Lorenzo. He took off his robe and swept the powdered wig from his head. "Come along, Bannister. I am going to visit my brother."

Chapter Twenty-Seven

With Hawthorne on one side and Morgan on the other, Lorenzo headed back to the fort. The guards trailed behind them, muskets slung over their backs.

Lorenzo could understand how Hawthorne felt. To know that his missing brother was on his doorstep, but not to visit him? That was unthinkable. Still, he did not think it was a good idea, but he kept his worries to himself.

Hawthorne ground to a halt by the well inside Fort Charlotte. "Bring out the prisoner."

The guards left. Hawthorne stood with his arms crossed over his chest. Morgan stared at pigeons that had landed on the parade ground and were pecking at the ground. Lorenzo locked his gaze on the wooden door the guards had gone through.

In short order, Blackie ambled out accompanied by a marine.

"My God," Hawthorne whispered to Lorenzo as they approached. "That is Evan."

Head held high, Blackie looked solemn, like a man on his way to the gallows, until he caught a glimpse of Lorenzo. He smiled, apparently surprised to see him still alive. His gaze moved to Hawthorne. Blackie stopped a foot away from them and shot Lorenzo a questioning look.

Lorenzo waited for Hawthorne to say something. When it became obvious that emotion made that impossible, Lorenzo spoke. "It is my privilege to introduce Judge Robert Hawthorne. Judge Hawthorne, this is Dr. Black."

Blackie bowed. "It is an honor, sir." He straightened. "Robert Hawthorne?" he asked.

Hope sprang to Lorenzo's chest. Had Blackie finally remembered?

"Is this the man you told me about on the island?" Blackie asked. "I thought you two were mortal enemies."

Lorenzo's gaze slid to Hawthorne's. "We have buried the hatchet."

"Luckily," Hawthorne put in, "we did not bury it in each other's back."

"Blessed are the peacemakers," Blackie mumbled.

"Dr. Black," Hawthorne began, hand to chin, "you look familiar. I believe we have met before."

"I am sorry, sir," Blackie said. "If that is the case, I do not recall it."

"I am certain we have. Perhaps at Briar Crest, my estate in England?"

Blackie shook his head.

"I attended medical school at the University of Edinburgh. Perhaps we met there?"

Again, Blackie shook his head.

Lorenzo knew what Hawthorne was doing. He was hoping to jog Blackie's memory by hitting the high points of Evan's life.

Hawthorne continued on. "I once owned a plantation in Baton Rouge. Could we have met there?"

"I think you have me confused with someone else," Blackie said.

Hawthorne sighed. "Perhaps."

Lorenzo felt deeply sorry for Hawthorne. He had just fired his best shot and it had missed.

"Well, Dr. Black," Hawthorne said, clapping his hands together and rubbing them vigorously, "this is your lucky day. Dr. Bannister made a very good case for offering you parole. As I am in a particularly good mood today, I have decided to grant his request."

Blackie's eyes widened. "Thank you, sir."

"My assistant will present a page for your signature." At this point he gestured toward Morgan who snapped open the case and took out a piece of paper, ink, and a stoppered ink bottle. Morgan handed Blackie the page for his inspection.

Blackie read it, frowning from time to time. He looked at Lorenzo.

He nodded to indicate that it was an acceptable deal.

Blackie took the quill pen that Morgan offered, leaned over the portable desk, and signed "Dr. Black."

"You and Dr. Bannister may leave the first thing in the morning," Hawthorne said. "I would be honored if you would sup with me tonight."

"It would be my pleasure," Blackie said.

"What are you offering?" Lorenzo asked.

Hawthorne frowned at Lorenzo in consternation. "Does it matter?"

"Are you offering a better meal than the jail?"

Blackie reddened. "Please forgive my impetuous friend. Sometimes his mouth operates independent of his brain."

"Yes, I know," Hawthorne said. "If you will excuse me, Dr. Black. I need to speak to Dr. Bannister in private. Mr. Morgan, please see Dr. Black to my house."

Davy Morgan gave him a small salute. "It would be my pleasure, sir."

Lorenzo watched the two men walk away.

"I have found my brother," Hawthorne mumbled, "only to lose him again."

"You can come to New Orleans and visit him whenever you wish."

"There is the tiny matter of my banishment from Louisiana."

"I can talk Don Bernardo into lifting the order."

"There is another small matter we have not discussed. My life will be at jeopardy if I set foot in Louisiana. Some cad reserved the right to call me out for a duel when I was completely recovered."

Lorenzo reddened. "Well, all of us spout off from time to time and later regret it."

Hawthorne's eyes crinkled in amusement. He slowly stretched out his hand. "Let's bury the hatchet once and for all. Please accept my apologies for everything that has happened in the past."

"Apology accepted." Lorenzo clasped his hand and gave it a firm shake.

"Thank you, Lorenzo, for befriending my brother."

It was the first time Hawthorne had dropped his English stiffness and had used his first name. Lorenzo could not leave without warning Hawthorne and Davy that they were in danger.

"You should get out of Mobile as soon as possible."

"Why?" Hawthorne asked.

"Get out of Mobile."

Hawthorne tilted his head. "Are we in danger?"

"Get out of Mobile."

Hawthorne seemed to understand that Lorenzo had said all he could say. "Thank you, my friend."

"I have a question. How many of you are there?"

"Pardon me?"

"How many more Hawthornes are going to cross my path?"

"I have six brothers."

Lorenzo groaned.

Hawthorne laughed and clamped a hand on Lorenzo's

shoulder. "I was joking. There are only three of us."

"You, Blackie and Dunstan?"

"No, Dunstan was a cousin. There is a brother you still haven't met." Hawthorne gave him an evil smile. "Hardly a comforting thought, eh?"

Chapter
Twenty-Eight

"Faster, faster!" Lorenzo said, bending over his horse's neck. Hooves pounded beneath him. Ahead, a plantation home on the outskirts of New Orleans blazed with candles in every window.

Tonight was New Year's Eve. Lorenzo knew exactly where Eugenie would be. Every year for as long as he had known her, she celebrated the holiday with Don Bernardo's in-laws, the Saint Maxents.

He slowed when he came to the guard standing by the main gate. He stopped and waited for Blackie to catch up with him.

The soldier on duty snapped to attention and saluted. "Good evening, Major."

"Evening." Lorenzo saluted in return, although he was not in uniform. "That man is with me." He pointed to Blackie a hundred yards back. "Assuming he ever catches up."

A few seconds later, Blackie reined in beside him.

The guard stepped back and let them pass.

"Lorenzo," Blackie said as they rode toward the mansion, "we can't go in dressed like this."

"Sure we can! No one will care. And if they do . . ." Lorenzo flipped his hand in a scornful gesture.

After being on the road all day, they were mud-splattered and reeked of horse sweat. Lorenzo had not seen Eugenie in a month. Formalities like a shave and a bath did not seem important.

Abercrombie, still nursing a wounded foot, remained in Mobile. Hawthorne had promised to take care of him until he was well enough to serve aboard a ship. Lorenzo feared the gunshot would leave the lad with a permanent limp.

Lorenzo bounded down from his horse and handed his reins to a little boy named Pedro.

"Welcome back, Major," Pedro said, his face shining with joy.

"Pedro! How goes it?"

"Never better!"

People drinking champagne milled about on the lawn. Lorenzo searched for Eugenie, but did not see her.

"Are you looking for Mrs. Bannister?" Pedro asked.

"Where is she?"

"Not sure, but she's around somewhere."

Lorenzo bounded up the brick steps to the front door. It stood wide open.

Music filtered from an inside room where a string quartet

was playing. Servants were everywhere offering canapés on silver trays.

The butler, who should have announced Lorenzo, merely stared at him open-mouthed as if he were a ghost risen from the dead.

Héctor, standing with a pretty young woman and an older woman, was the first to notice him. Absolute joy spread on his face. He spoke to his companions, no doubt asking their permission to leave, and rushed over to Lorenzo. He grabbed Lorenzo by the upper arms. "*Madre de Dios*, am I glad to see you! Now I don't have to set sail on the Eversink."

"What are you talking about?"

"*Mi hijo!*" Gálvez called from across the room. He separated himself from a cluster of men in dress uniforms and hurried forward. "Welcome back."

He pulled Lorenzo to him in a Spanish-style embrace, each man slapping the other's back. The general pushed back, noticed dirt on his uniform as a result of the embrace, and dusted it off.

Lorenzo handed him the Parole for Prisoner Exchange. "I ran into a little trouble, sir."

Gálvez read the document. "I'll make sure two prisoners of war are released and sent to Mobile on the morrow."

"Thank you, Your Excellency. Where's Eugenie?"

The general looked around. "She was here a moment ago. She said something about going to the kitchen."

Lorenzo started to go, but found Gálvez holding his arm.

"What news do you bring from Havana?"

"Navarro and Bonet refuse to help, sir. You are on your own if you attack Mobile."

Gálvez looked straight at Blackie, who still stood on the threshold by the butler. "Who, pray tell, is that?"

"A pirate I ran into on the Liberty. It's a long story, sir. You mind if I fill you in on the details later? I'd like to see Eugenie."

Gálvez held him in an iron grip. "The Liberty?"

"Yes. He was quartermaster."

"Where is the captain?"

"Dead, Your Excellency. May I go, please?"

The general refused to release him. "What is your pirate's name?"

"Evan Black."

On the way to New Orleans, they had discussed first names. Blackie had rejected them all until, in a bold stroke, Lorenzo suggested "Evan." Blackie had liked it. To Lorenzo's disappointment, it had not brought back any memories.

"That's the man in the portrait," Gálvez whispered. "That's Hawthorne's brother."

"You're wrong, sir," Lorenzo lied as he tried to peel away his fingers. "That man is Dr. Evan Black."

Gálvez frowned. "You are lying, Lorenzo. Why?"

"Trust me, sir. I'll explain later."

The general released him. "Find Eugenie, but report back to me. It is imperative that we have a long chat with your so-called Dr. Black."

"As you wish, sir." Lorenzo dashed through the main salon, pushing past people, saying, "Sorry, excuse me, pardon me," when he wanted to yell, "Get the heck out of my way!" He rushed through the back door and bolted down the brick sidewalk that led to the detached kitchen. It made sense to separate the kitchen from the rest of the house and avoid a fire hazard, but at the moment, the extra distance to Eugenie was extremely annoying.

He found her sitting all alone on a park bench in the Saint Maxent gardens behind the mansion. She wore a green silk ball gown, his favorite.

"I am looking for Mrs. Bannister," he said, walking toward her.

Eugenie squealed. She jumped up and ran to his open arms. He hugged her tight and kissed her over and over. It felt good to have her in his arms again. He pushed back and studied her face. As always, she was breathtakingly gorgeous. He felt as stupid and dull-witted as the day they met. He could not put two sensible sentences together.

"I have something to tell you!" French bubbled out of her as it always did when she was excited. "I'm going to have a baby!"

He stared at her a moment. "What?"

"A baby. I'm going to have a baby."

His throat went dry. "A baby? A boy or a girl?"

She socked him lightly on the arm. "Now how would I know that?"

"A baby?"

She nodded excitedly.

He hugged her tight. He pushed back. "*Mon dieu*, I shouldn't do that! Not in your delicate condition."

She gave him a light cuff on the chest. "Don't treat me like a china doll. I am not going to break."

They sat on the park bench and talked, catching up on all that had gone on since he left. Lorenzo had missed the birthday party for Don Bernardo's wife on December 27th. Because Lorenzo was delayed in returning from Havana, Don Bernardo had tapped Lieutenant Colonel Miró to head to Havana to negotiate with Bonet and Navarro. Even so, the general was planning to set sail on January 10th, no matter what.

A deep voice spoke at Lorenzo's back. It belonged to Héctor Calderón. "The general wishes to speak to you."

"Tell the general that I am busy and he can—"

"Yes, Major?"

Lorenzo cringed. It was General Gálvez's voice. "Tell the general that I am never too busy—" He glanced around and tried to look surprised to see the general standing behind him in the company of Major Calderón and Blackie.

The general and Major Calderón burst out laughing while Blackie merely smiled and shook his head.

"I regret interrupting such a happy scene," the general said, "but I need to speak with you urgently."

Flushed with embarrassment, Lorenzo stood up.

"I don't believe we've met," Eugenie said, smiling at Blackie.

"I'm sorry," Gálvez said. "Madame Bannister, this is Dr. Black."

She offered her hand. "*Enchantée.*"

Blackie bent over it and kissed her knuckles. "It is a pleasure to meet you."

"Dr. Black knows the location of a chest I seek," Gálvez said. "Major Bannister, I want you to retrieve it."

Lorenzo thought fast. "Sir, I respectfully request that you send Major Calderón."

Héctor made an ugly face at Lorenzo.

"Look, sir," Lorenzo said, "after being on a pirate ship—"

"A privateer," Blackie corrected.

Lorenzo ignored him. "And being in a sea battle with the English and being shipwrecked and taken prisoner—"

"The fleet sails on January 10th," Gálvez said. "I need that chest. It contains $20,000 in gold, funds for the expedition to Mobile. I want you and Dr. Black to go to Isla Mujeres, dig up the chest, and bring it to me. It is an easy assignment. What could go wrong?"

"What could go wrong?" Lorenzo echoed in dismay. "I could run into pirates, sir! Or the British. Or sharks! Or a hurricane! The possibilities are endless!"

Laughing, Gálvez turned and walked away.

About the Author

Lila Guzmán is a co-author of the award winning *Lorenzo Series* set during the American Revolution. *Lorenzo and the Turncoat*, the third book in the series, won the 2006 Arizona Authors Award. Her latest children's novel is *Kichi in Jungle Jeopardy* (Blooming Tree Press, 2006), the tale of a chihuahua lost in the Mayan jungle. She lives in Round Rock, Texas, and enjoys making school visits.

Contact her at lorenzo1776@yahoo.com and visit her on the web at www.lilaguzman.com.

Rick Guzmán practices law in Central Texas. With his wife, he co-wrote the Lorenzo series—young adult novels about the Spanish contribution to the American Revolution. A biography series on famous Latinos débuted in 2006 and includes *George López: Comedian and Television Star*. Rick and Lila have three grown children. He served as an artillery officer in the army.

Contact Rick at rguzman@rickguzmanlaw.com.

Acknowledgements

We owe a huge debt of gratitude to a number of people and organizations:

- The B & N critique group for reading *Lorenzo and the Pirate* and making it a better book. Many thanks to Sheryl Witschorke, Madeline Smoot, Carla Birnberg, Jan Ball, Maria Graziani, and Deborah Mussett.
- Special thanks to Mahani Zubedy for helping Lorenzo climb a coconut tree.
- The critique group that meets in Rick's law office: Ashley Vining, Lin Harris, and Stefanie Morris.
- Re-enactors and historical interpreters of the Spanish Louisiana Regiment.
- Mimi Lozano, editor of *Somos Primos*, for being a dear friend and a fount of encouragement.
- Wesley Odom, President of the Pensacola SAR, and J. M. Hochstetler, author of *Wind of the Spirit*, Book 3 of the *American Patriot Series*, for endorsing Lorenzo and the Pirate.
- The Texas Connection to the American Revolution, Granaderos de Gálvez, and other historical groups for moral support and the answers to dozens of questions.
- Carnival Cruise Line for taking us to Cozumel so we could tromp through the jungle and imagine what it must be like

to be shipwrecked on a small island.

- Special thanks to the United States Navy for teaching Lila celestial navigation and other seafaring skills. Several incidents in the novel are based on true events from her days as an officer of the line in Newport, Rhode Island, and Division Officer at the Defense Language Institute.

- And finally, the State of Alabama and the City of Mobile for a replica of Fort Charlotte, the British fort where Blackie and Lorenzo were jailed.